RIGHT THING

Stephanie Perry Moore

RIGHT THING

Morgan Love Series
Book 4

MOODY PUBLISHERS
CHICAGO

All Scripture quotations are taken from the *New King James Version*. Copyright © 1982 by Thomas Nelson, Inc. Used by permission. All rights reserved.

Edited by Kathryn Hall
Interior design: Ragont Design
Cover design and image: TS Design Studio
Author photo: Bonnie Rebholz
Word Searches by Pam Pugh

Some definitions found at the end of chapters are from WordSmyth.net.

Library of Congress Cataloging-in-Publication Data

Moore, Stephanie Perry.
    Right thing / Stephanie Perry Moore.
      p. cm. — (Morgan Love series ; #4)
    Summary: As she enters third grade, Morgan has some challenging times when she is tempted to disobey or break rules, but with the help of some of her friends—and prayers--she manages to improve. Educational exercises provided at the end of each chapter.
    ISBN 978-0-8024-2266-8
    [1. Conduct of life—Fiction. 2. Obedience—Fiction. 3. Schools—Fiction. 4. Friendship—Fiction. 5. Christian life—Fiction. 6. African Americans—Fiction.] I. Title.
    PZ7.M788125Ri 2011
    [Fic]—dc22

                                          2011000093

Printed by Bethany Press in Bloomington, MN – 06/11

1 3 5 7 9 10 8 6 4 2

Printed in the United States of America.

For
My Maternal Aunt
GussieMae Roundtree Bates
(Born February 13, 1960)

Of all my relatives, you were the one who has cheered me
on since the start. You got behind my work when most
weren't sure what I was doing. Thank you for reminding
me that getting the books out there may be hard,
but it's worth it. You told me that though I'd like many to
read my books, I need to concentrate more on the fact that
I'm blessing people by what I write. I pray every reader
focuses on pleasing God. Because following His plan for
their life is the only *right thing* that matters!

Contents

Chapter 1

Some Good

"No, Morgan, you are not going to watch that scary movie. It's not allowed in our home and you know that," my mother said firmly.

"Oh, come on, Mrs. Randall," Brooke begged. "Pleeeease. It'll be all right."

"No, sweetheart. It won't be all right. As I said, Morgan is not allowed to watch certain types of programs. I **recommend** you guys pick something else to watch. I want you girls to have a good time, but the rules are the rules. Morgan thinks she can handle those creepy movies, but she can't."

I went up to Mom and placed my arm around her waist to soften her up. "I can handle them, Mommy. I promise. I won't be afraid."

She stepped back from me, like I had a bad cold or something. "There's more to it, Morgan. That movie is rated PG-13 and it has scenes in it that you aren't ready to see yet."

"But my mom lets me watch them at home. And Morgan and I are the same age. Please, Mrs. Randall," Brooke pleaded again.

"No, girls. I said no and that's final," Mom said in her strong voice.

Both Brooke and I stomped off in a huff. We stomped hard. We were too upset at the moment to be respectful.

"You know what. Come here," Mom said, not being too happy with us. "I'm glad that you're staying over tonight, Brooke. And your mom told me that I could speak to you like I speak to Morgan. You're in my house and she knows I care about you. So, you little ladies need to listen up good. You must be polite when an adult says no. It's not the end of the world. Just find something else to do. And if you girls don't hurry up and turn those frowns into smiles, I'm going to put you to work."

"Work? I cleaned up everything," I said to Mom, still frowning.

"No, that *Summer Bridges* book I bought for you to work in over the summer has several pages that you haven't done. How about you and Brooke go and do that. Come back to me after a while so I can check how much you've done."

"Yes, ma'am," I said, trying hard not to show her how unhappy I was.

When Brooke and I went to my room, Brooke complained, "Wow, I can't believe she won't let us watch the movie."

"I know. I'm sorry. I'm a big girl and I want her to quit acting like I'm a baby. She keeps treating me like I'm little and can't handle anything. It makes me so angry."

"Well, you have to show her that you're a big girl instead of just telling her."

Looking around my room for the workbook, I said, "What do you mean, Brooke?"

"Here's the deal. When she goes to sleep, we'll watch the movie anyway," Brooke said, as she spotted the workbook on my bookcase and handed it to me.

"Huh?"

"That's how I got my mom to let me watch them. At night I would watch a movie and in the morning when she woke up I would tell her all about it."

"She didn't get mad that you watched somethin' you weren't supposed to watch?"

Brooke looked at me and smiled. "Well, I never really asked her."

"What if we get caught?" I was really scared because the whole plan sounded so risky.

"If she's asleep, how is she gonna know?" Brooke said, giving me a slick look and a wink.

Shrugging my shoulders I said, "I don't know."

"Let's just get these pages over with," Brooke said, as she snatched the book away from me and opened it to the last page I'd done. "We'll have her all buttered up so when she goes to sleep, she'll never know."

I heard what my friend was saying and I didn't want Brooke to think staying over at my house was lame. I wanted her to know that I'm cool and so is my mom. But I should have known that Mom wouldn't let me do everything Brooke could do at her house. We were both growing up, and I just wished Mom would accept that.

But for now, there was only one problem for me. After Mom said no, I didn't think I should do something that she told me not to do. Then again, I couldn't help but wonder, *Would it really be that bad?*

I looked at the *Summer Bridges* book, and my mom was right. I did have a lot of pages left to finish and summer was nearly over. I was going back to school next week to be in the third grade! I was definitely not a baby anymore. The first page we turned to was about **homophones**.

"*H-o-m-o-p-h-o-n-e-s*. Homophones."

"Okay, what are homophones?" Brooke asked me.

"They are words that sound the same but mean something different. Like *your*, which means you own something. Or *you're*, which stands for 'you are.'"

Brooke said, "Oh, I get it. And like *two*, the number two and the word *too*, which means 'also' or 'very.'"

"Exactly. And you use the pronoun *their* when you're talking about more than one person. Or the word *there*, when you're talking about another location. Or the word *they're*, which is short for 'they are.' Whew!"

"Wow. Homophones are tricky."

"Yep."

Brooke looked at the workbook. "Here's a sentence: *They herd/heard that sailors leave their families and sail away.*" As she read aloud, we were both looking at the page. We knew we had to circle the correct choice from the underlined words. But I just put my head down.

"Daddy," I said quietly, as I started feeling sad.

Brooke could tell that I was thinking about him. "I'm sorry, Morgan. It's just a sentence," Brooke said, patting my shoulder.

"I know, but it makes me think about how much I miss my dad."

"Well, it's okay to think about him. I'll do the sentence. The answer is *heard,* which means to hear something. *Herd* means a group of animals."

"Yeah, that sounds right to me. Next sentence: *I did not have any sodas four/for months. Four* means the number and *for* means—"

"It means that *for* is the right one," Brooke said, as we laughed.

"Yep. Here's another one: *Children should always try to make the write/right choices.*"

"*Write* means to write something down, but *right* is the correct answer because it means the opposite of wrong. Right?" Brooke said, smiling. We really were enjoying learning homophones together.

We kept on laughing as we finished the lesson and

rushed downstairs to show my mom our work. She was pleased with what we had done. Then Mom helped us bake some cookies. With our treats in hand, we headed to the basement for our girls' night of fun.

After a while, Brooke tiptoed over to the stairs and whispered softly, "All the lights are off up there. Your parents are probably asleep now, so we can watch the movie. She's not gonna come downstairs."

I didn't follow my own **instincts** and say no to my buddy. I just let my friend turn the channel to the scary movie. We sat close together as the weird music began. Knowing it was the wrong thing to do, I could feel trouble coming.

Not long after the movie started and the actors' names came across the TV screen, the light in the room came on too. That scared us so bad that Brooke almost jumped into my lap. Was it the bad man from the movie coming to get us? No! It was worse.

Mom yelled out, "I know that's not the movie I told you not to watch! Morgan, turn that TV off! You girls go upstairs and get in the bed right now! I said move!"

I looked at my friend. Brooke looked at me. I hung my head low and clicked off the TV. Walking upstairs, I knew I was in trouble with my mom for sure. And it was bad.

• • • • •

"Morgan, I'm sorry," Brooke said, as we were lying in my bed.

I didn't even say anything to her.

Later that night, we were both tossing and turning. It was a mess. Neither one of us could sleep.

When I couldn't take it any longer, I sat up in the bed and said, "I thought she was asleep. But I knew it was wrong for me watch that anyway. And I knew I would get in trouble for it, but I went along with you."

"You could have told me to turn it off, Morgan. Don't get mad at me!"

"I'm not mad at you, Brooke," I said, knowing that my friend was right. But I really did do it because I wanted to please her, not because I wanted to watch the movie. Though I didn't have to go along with it, she didn't have to throw it in my face either.

"We're both in trouble. Okay?" said Brooke. "I feel so bad. I wanna go to your mom right now and tell her I'm sorry." Then she thought about it some more and added, "But in the morning when she's calmed down. Anyway, I'm in double trouble."

"What do you mean?" I asked.

"My mom doesn't let me watch those movies either."

"Then why did you tell my mom that she did?"

"Because I never asked my mom if I could and she doesn't even know I watch them. I guess she lets me because she never comes to check and see what I'm lookin' at in the middle of the night."

"Maybe after my mom talks to her, she'll start."

We both lay back in the bed and closed our eyes. When

we opened them again it was morning. All we could hear was the sound of my mom's loud voice.

"Girls, get up! Now!"

I looked over at the clock and it was only 7 a.m. It wasn't even a school day, and I wanted to argue. But, for sure, we didn't need to make it worse since we were already in trouble.

"Uh-oh, she sounds really mad. We'd better hurry up," Brooke said.

Getting out of the bed, I prayed, *Lord, I don't even deserve to pray to You because I was wrong. But can You make Mom not so mad, please?*

"Morgan, what's taking you so long? Come on!"

Mom had us follow her down to the laundry room. There were piles of freshly washed clothes waiting for us. "Okay, get to sorting. Brooke, you'll fold towels and pillow cases. Morgan, you can handle your jeans and shirts. Now get to work."

She didn't say anything more, but she didn't leave us in the room by ourselves either. My mom just quietly watched us. And her silence was worse than any words.

Finally, I turned around to her and said, "Mom, I'm sorry."

"Sorry for what, Morgan? Sorry that you got caught doing something I told you not to? Sorry that you didn't get to see the movie? What are you sorry for?"

"No, ma'am, I'm sorry that we **disobeyed** you in the first place."

"You're not sorry about that."

"Yes, I am."

"If I hadn't come downstairs, you would have kept watching the movie, right?"

"But even the music had me a little jumpy," I added.

"That's one of my points, Morgan. You think you're a big girl and I can see that you're growing up. But if you're not careful, you're going to do more harm than good. If you keep acting like you know better than me, you'll miss out on some good times. I promise you."

"What does that mean, Mom?"

"Girl. I'm so mad at you," she said, **gritting** her teeth. "And Brooke—"

"Yes, ma'am?" Brooke said.

"I want Morgan to have friends who can help her do the right thing. Not ones who talk her into doing something wrong. I know last night you were a part of the reason for her doing the wrong thing. And I have a problem with that. I'm not sure if you're the type of friend Morgan needs to be around because together the two of you are creating some bad habits."

I went over to my mom and threw my arms around her. "No, Mom, we're good for each other."

"Well, if you're good for each other, then why are you doing things that are so wrong?"

"It's my fault," Brooke said. "I didn't tell you the truth. I told you that my mom let me watch those movies, but she doesn't even know I watch them. I figured since you were asleep, you wouldn't—"

"Come and check on you," Mom said, finishing my friend's sentence.

"Right. Yes, ma'am."

"But, Brooke, that's no way to be, sweetheart. Even when adults don't catch you doing the wrong thing, God is always there watching you."

"I didn't even think about that," Brooke said, as her eyes started to tear. Mine were beginning to do the same.

"Exactly. You have to think about the consequences to your actions. Would God want you doing something wrong? There's a reason why those movies are rated the way they are. Neither one of you girls is thirteen. Without you even knowing it, whatever you're watching on TV gets into your spirit. Then when you're not even watching TV, you can get tense and nervous about things. And I want to help you avoid times like that. Instead, I want you to deposit positive memories in your life."

"You're gonna talk to my mom, aren't you?" Brooke said with her head down.

My mom lifted her chin and said, "No, sweetie, you are. You're a big girl. And because you're a big girl, I expect you to tell her what's going on. I want her to call me and let me know that you did the right thing. But if I don't get a phone call soon after you go home, then I'll tell her. It's not because I want you to get in trouble for this. It's because I don't want you to get in trouble for something worse than this. We need to be able to trust you young ladies. You all should hold each other **accountable**."

"Accountable?" I said, unsure of what that meant.

Mom said, "It means that you help each other do what's right so you'll never, ever do what's wrong. It's not good for you to break the rules, because God is not pleased with that kind of behavior. Do you understand?"

"Yes, ma'am."

"Now, finish folding these clothes. Then come on up and get some breakfast. I love you both, okay?"

"Yes, ma'am," we said again.

When Mom went upstairs, Brooke said, "I'm sorry, Morgan. I shouldn't have pushed you into doing something that was wrong. I really do care about you."

"It's okay. I'm sorry I didn't stand up to you and tell you that there's no way I was gonna disobey what my mom said. But at least we're learning right from wrong."

"Yeah. We've got to do better."

• • • • •

"Oh, so you got caught watching some bad movies?" Papa said to me. Jayden and I were staying the night since my parents were celebrating their two-year anniversary. I didn't like it when Mom told her parents on me, but I was wrong and I would have to own up to it sometime.

"Get off of her back," Mama said to Papa. "Morgan, now you know that was something you weren't supposed to do, right?"

"Yes, ma'am. I know when Mommy tells me not to do something that I shouldn't do it, Mama."

"Speaking of the TV, go and turn that thing off. Don't you hear all that lightning and thunder outside, young lady?"

I did hear a little bit of thunder, but I didn't think it was that bad. That was one thing I didn't like about coming over to my grandparents' house. You had to sit still and be quiet when it was storming outside. You couldn't even move. I didn't like that because it made me focus more on the storm than anything else. At least when I was watching TV, I wasn't worried about the loud crackling of the lightning bolts.

The next day I went to church with Mama and Papa. During service, we prayed for Miss May's niece because her son, Billy Wood, got struck by lightning. My face looked very serious and I felt my insides quaking.

"Billy Wood from my class?" I asked Papa, whispering loudly.

Papa shushed me and asked, "You know him?"

"Yes, Billy is my friend. He was in my class."

Then I started praying. *Lord, please let Billy be okay.*

Right after church, Papa asked me if I wanted to go to the hospital and see Billy. I remembered the hospital from a year ago when I had to go and visit my mom. She and baby Jayden weren't doing too well. Pretty soon they were okay and didn't have to stay too long. Since I was over it now, I told Papa we could go.

When we got to the hospital, Mama and Papa were talking to Billy's mom and his aunt. I found out that if you weren't the mom, dad, grandparents, or another close relative, you had to have a special pass to go into a patient's room. So I went and sat in the waiting room. There was a girl sitting next to the remote control. The TV was off but I wanted to turn it on and watch something.

"Excuse me, can I have the remote control?"

"No," she said, sounding angry.

I could tell she was a little older than me. I didn't know why she was being so mean. I had never done anything to her and didn't even know her. So I tried again.

"Can I please get the remote control?"

She stood up from her seat, walked over, and looked in my face. The remote control was still in the seat. She pushed me just a little and said, "I told you no the first time."

"You don't own the TVs in this hospital."

Before she could say anything back, Mama walked up and said, "Morgan, come on, sweetheart. They're going to let you see your friend."

"Okay."

"Why do you have that look on your face?" Mama asked.

I couldn't even give Mama an answer. But out of the corner of my eye, I could see the mean girl looking at me like, *HA, HA, HA! You didn't get the remote!* She even stuck her tongue out at me. I just shook it off. It wasn't that important to me and I didn't want to go into Billy's room upset about anything.

"They said you can go in for a little bit. He's awake and he just finished his lunch. He's going to be okay, honey."

I pushed open the door to see Billy sitting up with the TV on.

"Billy!"

"Hey, Morgan, you came to see me?"

"Yeah, and the whole church is praying for you. What happened?"

"I was in the garage and I was supposed to be sitting down. All I remember was I didn't want my bicycle to get wet. The next thing I knew, I woke up here. They said it could have been worse. But I'm cool."

"Oh, Billy. I'm glad you're okay."

"I love it! It's making my sister crazy mad that I'm getting all this **attention**."

"Your sister?"

"Yeah. My mom said she's in the waiting area. She's tall and always has a mean look on her face. Her name is Bridget."

"Yeah, I met her," I said, looking sad and mad all mixed up together like a peanut butter and jelly sandwich.

"Don't worry about her. She's not so tough. I did learn one thing, though. When your parents tell you to do something, just do it. Or, you could end up getting struck by lightning, or worse. Even though it knocked me out and I ended up in the hospital, I wasn't hurt too bad. So in the end, my nightmare turned out to have some good."

Letter to Dad

Dear Dad,

I learned some things that I can share with all kids. I **recommend** they do what their parents say. I learned that some words sound the same but are spelled different and have different meanings. And if you don't get the word right, you'll mess up a sentence. For example, plane and plain are **homophones**. I hope you get on a PLANE soon and come see me. My **instincts** tell me you'll be here before I know it.

Dad, I **disobeyed** Mom. I know it was wrong. Mom was gritting her teeth to hold in her anger. I know now that I must be **accountable** for my bad actions. She got my **attention** and I won't let her, you, Daddy Derek, Mama, Papa, or God down again.

Your daughter,
Learning Morgan

Word Search

```
H  A  T  T  E  N  T  I  V  R  B  A
D  I  S  O  B  E  Y  E  D  E  A  C
J  B  L  E  W  A  S  E  E  C  K  I
G  B  L  U  E  T  E  K  C  O  E  N
D  R  V  R  Y  T  A  O  X  M  I  S
I  Z  I  L  E  E  U  W  W  M  N  T
S  F  F  T  R  N  O  E  E  E  S  I
O  L  L  D  T  T  J  A  E  N  T  N
B  E  U  A  F  I  G  K  K  D  I  C
Y  W  B  A  C  O  N  J  O  H  N  T
D  L  P  H  O  N  E  G  A  M  C  S
E  H  O  M  O  P  H  O  N  E  S  L
```

ACCOUNTABLE

ATTENTION

DISOBEYED

GRITTING

HOMOPHONES

INSTINCTS

RECOMMEND

Words to Know and Learn

1) **rec·om·mend** (rĕk'ə-mĕnd') *verb*
To present as worth doing; suggest; advise.

2) **hom·o·phone** (hŏm'ə-fōn', hō'mə-) *noun*
A word that is pronounced the same as another but has a different
meaning and often a different spelling, such as night, knight, blue, blew.

3) **in·stinct** (ĭn'stĭngkt') *noun*
A strong natural tendency or ability.

4) **dis·o·bey** (dĭs'ə-bā') *verb* **dis·o·beyed** (past tense)
To refuse or fail to follow an order or rule.

5) **grit·ting** (grĭt) *verb*
Clamping (the teeth) together.

6) **ac·count·a·ble** (ə-koun'tə-bəl) *adjective*
To be held responsible for one's actions.

7) **at·ten·tion** (ə-tĕn'shən) *noun*
Concentration of the mind on something.

Chapter 2

Never Bad

"No, oh, no!" I moaned, as I looked at the third grade classroom lists outside the school's office door. I was in for some trouble now.

"What's wrong with you? Are you kiddin' me? Third grade is about to be awesome. We're in the same class again," Brooke said, as she walked up beside me and grabbed my shoulders.

She and I were both excited to be in the same class again. It was going to be cool because Trey Spencer and Alec London were our classmates too. I smiled as I pointed to both their names.

"Wait, so you're happy Alec's in our class?"

"Yeah, he's cool. And I know you're happy Trey's in our class," I teased Brooke.

"Yeah, Trey is my buddy. So if the class is cool, what's your problem?"

"Mrs. Hardy is our teacher and you know they say she's mean."

"Oh, my goodness, that's right. I'm sad now," Brooke said.

"Well, at least y'all have each other," a voice behind us said. It was Chanté. "I got Miss Harper and I would take Mrs. Hardy any day to be in the class with you all."

Everyone wants the first day of school to be bubbly and bright. But I couldn't help but remember that this time last year my world was upside down! Right before school started, my dad went back to the Navy. My mom was having a new baby. I also had a new daddy to get used to. But Daddy Derek turned out to be okay after all. Baby Jayden isn't too bad either. Besides, I have good friends now at this school. I just hoped this year was going to be even better.

I was hoping to start the third grade off on the right track. But Mrs. Hardy? Ughh! She was the one who yelled in the hallway at everybody else's class. She's the one who makes her class come in early from recess. She's the one who doesn't let her class talk that much at lunchtime. She's the one everyone prays they don't have as a teacher.

I had everything going on with me this week—from getting into trouble to visiting Billy in the hospital. But I forgot to pray that I wouldn't have Mrs. Hardy!

"You're makin' a big deal out of nothin'," Brooke said. "She can't be that bad."

"I hope you're right," I said to my friend. Then I looked

over at Chanté and said, "Smile, girl. I think our classes are right next to each other."

"They are," Chanté said. "But I don't have anyone I know in mine. Even Billy is in your class. I saw his name on Mrs. Hardy's list."

"Guess what, guys. I saw Billy in the hospital this weekend. I don't think he's comin' to school today."

"That's right. My mom told me that he was hurt. I hope he's okay. I can't believe he got struck by lightning," Chanté said to us.

"Me either. Whenever there's a storm, I'm gonna sit still. I definitely won't be going outside," I said to them.

"Well, you all aren't in my class, but you're still my girls. Right?" Chanté asked, as Brooke and I nodded our heads. "Good, then that's all that matters."

"Girls, get into your classrooms. The bell is just about to ring," said a lady we never met before. "Let's move it right now."

I looked at Brooke. Brooke looked at me. Chanté darted away to her class. Right then, I knew Mrs. Hardy was as mean as everyone said she was. It was going to be a long year.

"Let's stick together," Brooke whispered to me.

"I don't even think so because I've given the class assigned seats. Find your name on the desk and park it there," she said from behind us.

"It looks like the milk in her cereal must have been spoiled this morning or somethin'," Alec whispered from in front of me.

Our names were listed in alphabetical order by last name. Morgan Love followed Alec London. Brooke was a couple of rows over in the front of the class. Her last name was Atwater so she wasn't near me. She really didn't like that she wasn't sitting by Trey. Since his last name was Spencer, his seat was in the back of the room.

Mrs. Hardy stood in the front of the room, looked down at us from the top of her glasses, and said "Good morning, class."

"Good morning," we all said, not sounding too happy.

"I see a lot of you have long faces this morning. I've also been walking around the halls hearing all the students say, 'Oh, I'm glad I don't have Mrs. Hardy. She's so mean.' Well, let me just say this. If you are a good student, we won't have any problems. Yes, I am hard on my class, but my students leave the third grade passing the **mandatory** test. It is a standard reading and math test that students must pass to go on to the fourth grade. If not, you could have me again. And that seems to be a big reason for everybody to work hard and move on."

"Why are you so mean?" Trey blurted out.

"First of all, people don't follow my rules. By the way, the rules are posted next to the door. And, young man, you just broke rule number one. If you want to be heard in my class, you have to raise your hand. I can't just let you do what you want to do. There must be order in my class. We will have fun when it's time. But we have a lot to learn in the next ten months. Enough said. If you show honesty,

integrity, and respect in my classroom at all times, we won't have any problems. I very well may be your favorite teacher by the end of it all."

Everybody started laughing. Who was going to believe that?

"This is very serious. And for those of you who laughed, just remember I know each of your faces. Trust me, you don't want to get on my bad side. Now that we've got that out of the way, let's get busy. What was the best thing you remember about your summer break? We'll start up here," she said, pointing to Brooke.

Brooke answered, "Well, for me, I remember my birthday party. All my friends came and it was a special time. I know a lot of you guys weren't invited but that's because I didn't know you. Next summer, I'll invite everybody and we'll have a super time."

More kids talked about their parties. Some kids talked about visiting with their families out of town. After everyone finished, I raised my hand to speak.

"Hi, I'm Morgan Love. Like Brooke Atwater, I only know a couple of you guys in here. Trey, Alec, and Brooke. I know Billy too, but he's not here today. I also had a great time with some of my cousins. I found out this summer that I have good self-esteem. Nobody is perfect, but we're all amazing just the way we are."

"Okay, Morgan. That was very good," Mrs. Hardy said. "All right, class. Now we can break into groups and have some fun."

The rest of the day we played games and did work-sheets on things we should know up to this point. I watched as Mrs. Hardy walked around, getting to know all of my classmates. Even though she was a serious teacher, I realized she had a heart too.

So I prayed, *Lord, I'm sorry that I really didn't want to have Mrs. Hardy when I came to her class. I've gotta have more faith that You know what's best. She doesn't seem like a bad lady. I love You, Lord. And I hope to have a great year in the third grade.*

● ● ● ● ●

After we'd been in school for a week, Mrs. Hardy was so pleased with our conduct that she let us choose our own seats. Alec moved to the back and sat next to Trey. And since I had an open seat next to me, Brooke came and sat in it.

When everyone finished changing their seats, Mrs. Hardy said, "Some classes don't start learning their multi-plication facts until the tenth week. But I want us to get an early start on things. How many of you want an early start?"

All of us raised our hands. "Okay, we will have to cut five minutes of recess and come inside to do extra math drills. In a few weeks, we're going to have a big test to see who's doing well and who needs after-school **tutoring**."

Brooke and I looked at each other. Then we looked all around the classroom. From the faces I saw, it looked like no one wanted to be in after-school tutoring. Not that getting extra help was a bad thing, but for us it wasn't good. We were going to pass this test!

"Well then, let's get started. Last week, we worked on 1s and 0s. Now we'll do the 2s, 3s, and 4s."

Trey raised his hand. "Yes, sir, Mr. Spencer?"

"Mrs. Hardy, I just don't understand why you have 2 + 2 on the board if we're doing multiplication."

"Okay, Trey. What's 2 + 2?"

"It's 4."

"And 3 + 3?"

"Six."

"And 4 + 4?"

"It's 8."

"Now, look at this. 2 + 2 is 4, but that's the same thing as 2x2. You're just adding the number 2 two times."

"Huh?" Trey was confused and many of us were as well. I noticed there were tons of puzzled looks.

Alec said, "I think I get it. If 2x2 is 4, then 2x3 is 6, because you're adding the number 3 two times."

"Exactly. So Alec, since Trey just told us 4 + 4 is 8, what's 2x4?"

"Eight."

"And what's 2x5?"

"Ten."

"And 2x6?"

"Twelve. And you know that because 6 + 6 is 12 and 5 + 5 is 10."

"Great!"

"And we only have to go to 12?" Brooke shouted out. "Oh, I'm sorry, Mrs. Hardy."

The teacher looked sternly at her for not raising her hand and Brooke got the message.

"Yes, Brooke. We have to go up to 12. So what's 2x12?"

"Twenty-four!" we shouted.

"Very good, class. Now we have to learn the 3s."

She wrote 2 + 2 + 2 on the board. Again, we all kind of looked like, *What is this?* Multiplication wasn't gonna be so easy to learn.

"Alec, what's 2 + 2 + 2?"

Alec quickly answered, "Six."

"Okay, so when you add the number 2 three times it equals 6 as well. Then 3 + 3 + 3 is 9 and 3x3 is 9. The more you write the facts down, the easier it becomes to remember them. You'll get a lot of practice as you do your homework assignments."

We went on to do the rest of the 3s:

3x4 is 12; 3x5 is 15; 3x6 is 18; 3x7 is 21; 3x8 is 24; 3x9 is 27; 3x10 is 30; 3x11 is 33; 3x12 is 36.

The 4s were easy too:

4x1 is 4; 4x2 is 8; 4x3 is 12; 4x4 is 16; 4x5 is 20; 4x6 is 24; 4x7 is 28; 4x8 is 32; 4x9 is 36; 4x10 is 40; 4x11 is 44; 4x12 is 48.

The 5s were simple to remember.

"I know you guys know how to do your 5s. Just count by 5 up to 12. Ready?"

Mrs. Hardy clapped her hands to a beat and we clapped with her: "5, 10, 15, 20, 25, 30, 35, 40, 45, 50, 55, 60."

"See, you just have to go to 12. The 10s are just as easy. Any number times 10 is that same number but add a 0: 10x1 is 10; 10x2 is 20; 10x3 is 30; 10x4 is 40; 10x5 is 50; 10x6 is 60; 10x7 is 70; 10x8 is 80; 10x9 is 90; 10x10 is 100; 10x11 is 110; 10x12 is 120."

Alec raised his hand. "Mrs. Hardy, I like the 10s."

"That's good, Alec. I like the 11s myself. Any number times 11 is the number twice."

"The number twice? Oh, I'm sorry again, Mrs. Hardy," Brooke said. She kept forgetting to raise her hand.

"Brooke, you have to understand. If you want to speak, you must always raise your hand."

"Sorry."

"It means you will get the answer by repeating the same number you are multiplying by 11. For example, 2x11 is 22; 3x11 is 33; 4x11 is 44."

"Oh, so 5x11 is 55 and 6x11 is 66?"

"Exactly. It's a little tricky when you get to the numbers 11 and 12, but we'll discuss that when we get there."

All of that fun learning took up the first hour of class. In the second hour, Mrs. Hardy called Alec and me to her desk.

"Are the two of you aware of the Challenge Program? This is a special class that offers students with high grades a chance to learn faster. A letter was sent to your parents about your participation and they have given you both permission."

Mom and Daddy Derek told me about it and I guess it was going to be okay. But I told them that I still didn't want to skip a grade if that was a part of it. Before I could say anything to Mrs. Hardy, Alec spoke up.

"Yeah, they got it. It's a program that challenges kids to work a little harder," Alec said, seeming more **astute** than I'd ever heard him sound before.

"That is correct. You will be taking a bus to another school one day a week and stay there the remainder of that day. I'm really proud of you both. You're my only Challenge students this year. If you have any difficulty with the lessons, let me know. My kids have a **reputation** in Challenge of being leaders, so I expect only the best from both of you, okay?" Mrs. Hardy asked, waiting on a positive answer from us.

"Yes, ma'am," we said.

Looking pleased and smiling, she said, "Good, then go ahead and gather your things. The bus is waiting for you."

On the way to the bus, I must have looked at Alec like I had a question mark on my face. He already knew what I was thinking because he said, "Oh, what? You didn't think I was smart, huh?"

"I mean, last year you barely did any work."

"That was different. I was goin' through some stuff at home and I didn't try hard. You know what I'm talkin' about. But the school I used to attend was a lot harder than this one. I guess it got me ready for the program. People say this Challenge Program is real hard. So if we need to study together, we should ask our parents if it's okay with them," Alec suggested.

"Yeah, that'll be fun."

"Yeah, that'll be fun," some girl behind us mocked, as we walked through the hallway.

She stuck out her leg and when he saw I was about to trip, Alec grabbed my arm. I looked at her real hard. I knew that girl. It was Billy's sister, Bridget. Alec and I didn't pay any attention to her and just went outside to get on the bus.

"I don't know why she's so bad and why she's so mean to me," I said.

"Maybe something's bothering her and she's mad about it. Don't even worry about it. Let's go check out this new program."

We both jumped up on the bus, ready and **eager** to learn.

• • • • •

"What's wrong with Brooke?" Chanté asked me on the playground.

We'd been in school for four weeks. I was finding out that the third grade was not a joke. I had to study harder than ever before. Although I only went to the Challenge Program once a week, I already had a report to turn in. Alec thought he needed to study with me because we had a test coming up in a week. But I was thinking that I might have to study with him. He was making nothing but 100s.

Even though I had all As because I worked hard at it, it reminded me how really happy I was that my mom hadn't let me skip a grade. This was enough of a challenge for me. Today was the big multiplication test. Our teacher was going to time us on our 2s, 3s, 4s, 5s, 10s, and 11s facts. We couldn't just know them; we had to be able to recall them quickly.

I was ready! Over the last two weeks, Mom, Daddy Derek, Mama, and Papa tested me with flash cards. Mom even put the cards in Jayden's hand and taught him how to turn it over and show me the right answer. I couldn't believe he was already a one-year-old and walking up a storm. The time had gone by so fast.

Chanté and I headed over to Brooke by the swings. When she saw us coming, Brooke turned her head. She twisted the swing around so we couldn't see her face. She'd been acting weird all day, so I knew something was wrong.

"Are you crying?" Chanté asked her, as she went around the swing to look at Brooke's face.

"Leave me alone, Chanté. Don't make a big deal about it. Okay?"

"What's going on, Brooke? Did Trey do somethin' to you, girl?" Chanté asked.

"No, nobody did anything. I'm just not a smart girl. I don't even **deserve** to have any friends."

Chanté just looked at me like she didn't know what else to say. I walked in front of Brooke and said, "Talk to me, Brooke. Tell me what's wrong."

"You don't care."

"I wouldn't be askin' you if I didn't care. That's not fair."

Brooke blurted out, "I didn't study for the test! Okay?"

"What test do y'all have?" Chanté asked. "Mrs. Hardy must be much harder because we don't have any test this week."

I knew what she was talking about so I explained to Chanté, "We have a big multiplication test today . . . and our teacher is cool. She's just tryin' to help us stay ahead."

Brooke rolled her eyes and said, "I don't wanna be ahead. We're moving too fast. I thought the test was next week."

"Brooke, how could you think it was next week? She's been tellin' us all along that the test would be today. You knew. Why didn't you study?" I wasn't letting her off the hook.

Chanté said, "I don't even know my times tables yet."

I just shook my head, thinking, *This is not the time to say that. Brooke was already saying she didn't know hers either.*

She surprised me when she stood up from the swings and grabbed my shirt. "Morgan, you gotta help me! Please? I need you now, bad. You can't let me fail."

"Help you how? You wanna go over them with my

flash cards? We still have ten minutes before we have to go back inside. And I can bring them to lunch if you want."

"No," Brooke said, as she got even closer and started whispering. "You know . . . we sit right beside each other, right?"

"And?"

"And . . . I just thought—Oh, forget it! You don't care about me."

"Whatever," Chanté said. "You know Morgan would help you with anything that you need."

"I'm just sayin' this one time, Morgan. I promise I'll study this weekend and from now on for every test. If I fail, I'll be in super trouble for not studying. Besides, if I have to do after-school tutoring, I won't have anyone to pick me up because my mom works. And kids will laugh at me. I need your help, Morgan, please!"

"Calm down, Brooke. Just tell her what you need and she'll help you," Chanté said.

"Your teacher is calling you to come inside," I said to Chanté. I saw her class lining up.

"See, you act like you don't even wanna help me," Brooke said and walked away in a hurry.

I was confused so I just plopped down on the swing she left empty. During lunch, Brooke didn't sit beside me. I guess I looked kinda out of it when I took my tray because Alec came right behind me and tried to cheer me up.

"I see Brooke didn't sit with you at lunch. You must have told her no."

"About what?" I wondered what he meant.

Surprising me, he said, "She wants to copy off of your math test."

I almost dropped my tray. So that was it!

"How do you know?"

"Because I heard Trey giving her the stupid idea."

"I really didn't know what she wanted, but now it all makes sense. She kept saying we sit right beside each other. Ughh! I can't do that," I told Alec.

"You can't and you shouldn't. But will you?"

Alec left me standing there thinking. After that, I didn't even want to go to class. Before I was eager for the test but now the last thing I wanted was to take that test. I didn't want my best friend to fail, but letting her cheat off my test was just wrong.

My mom had already told us that we had to be there to help each other do the right thing. Brooke wanted me to help her cheat. There was no way I was going to do it.

Soon after Mrs. Hardy told us to begin the test, she stepped out of the classroom. Tears started to fall from Brooke's eyes and she hit the empty test paper. Feeling sorry for her, I just pushed my test over a little. That way if she wanted to copy, she could.

Then she whispered, "Thank you so much, Morgan. I will study next time. I promise. Helping a friend out is never bad."

Letter to Dad

Dear Dad,

Well, since school is **mandatory**, I guess I should have a good attitude about it. I'm in the 3rd grade now. And my teacher says if we all work hard, treat each other right, and have **integrity**, we'll do fine in her class. But 3rd grade is more challenging for me. I may need **tutoring**.

For now, I have all As. Mom says I'm real **astute**. I have a **reputation** of studying hard every day. I guess I'm **eager** to learn more than I know. I do want to make you and Mom proud. I can't wait to see you, Dad. Come home soon. You **deserve** a big hug for all your service to our country.

Your daughter,
Hard-working Morgan

Word Search

```
S  M  A  R  T  R  H  T  B  A  K  E
E  M  K  N  G  E  E  U  E  I  D  A
R  D  A  G  X  P  L  T  G  N  I  S
V  R  M  N  H  U  P  E  C  T  N  T
E  B  E  I  D  T  E  V  T  E  T  U
E  E  R  R  E  A  D  L  O  G  E  T
A  A  I  O  S  T  T  M  O  R  G  E
G  V  C  T  E  I  Q  O  T  I  A  N
E  E  A  U  R  O  K  P  R  T  L  S
R  R  J  T  V  N  L  A  N  Y  O  P
Q  U  I  Z  E  T  E  A  C  H  E  R
N  E  C  E  S  S  A  R  Y  D  A  Y
```

ASTUTE

DESERVE

EAGER

INTEGRITY

MANDATORY

REPUTATION

TUTORING

Words to Know and Learn

1) **man·da·to·ry** (măn'də-tôr'ē, -tōr'ē) *adjective*
Required.

2) **in·teg·ri·ty** (ĭn-tĕg'rĭ-tē) *noun*
A strong sense of honesty; firmness of moral character.

3) **tu·tor·ing** (tū'tər, tyū'-) *verb*
Instruct or teach privately.

4) **as·tute** (ə-stūt', ə-styūt') *adjective*
Being shrewd; quick in understanding or judgment.

5) **rep·u·ta·tion** (rĕp'yə-tā'shən) *noun*
The level of respect at which a person is thought of by others.

6) **ea·ger** (ē'gər) *adjective*
Having or showing keen interest, intense desire, or impatient expectancy.

7) **de·serve** (dĭ-zûrv') *verb*
To be worthy of or have a right to.

Chapter 3

No Warmth

"You gotta let me see! I can't see it," Brooke was whispering to me. My conscience was making me inch my paper back from the edge of my desk.

I cared about my friend, I did. But honestly, it wasn't right to let her copy from me. Maybe my helping her wasn't doing her any good. Just maybe she needed to fail to prove that you have to study to make good grades the right way. This reminded me of what we learned in Miss Nelson's class last year about cause and effect. Since Brooke didn't study, she would get a bad grade.

But I felt sorry for her and I slid my paper over on my desk to where she could see it again. I knew I wasn't really helping her, but I did it anyway.

"You'd better look out!" someone from the back hissed.

That just made me feel worse. I mean, how many people knew I was doing something that I wasn't supposed to? I pulled my paper back to the center of my desk. And as soon as I looked up, Mrs. Hardy was halfway to me. Oh, my goodness! She was looking at me and I was going to be in trouble. Maybe I should get in trouble but I sure didn't want to. I didn't do this because I really wanted to. I did it because I thought I could help Brooke.

With each step she took, I started feeling sick and my head was hurting. I was sweating all over. Her eyes were squinted just like she knew I was doing something I wasn't supposed to.

Just when I thought I was caught, someone from the back of the room started acting crazy! A kid was standing on a chair, jumping up and down. I couldn't look back to see exactly who it was because I was in a panic. Upset by what she saw, Mrs. Hardy took her eyes off me. Whoever was cutting up was in big trouble.

She went right past me and straight to the back of the room.

"Alec London, you know that is not called for. Get down off of that chair right now!" she said loudly.

Everybody started laughing at him and I wondered why he was doing it. When she made him follow her outside, he looked over at me and smiled. Then I knew that he made a big scene just to save me. But why? I couldn't wait to ask him. But right now he was in trouble.

Of course when Mrs. Hardy left the room with Alec, the

class wasn't quiet. Everyone was imitating Alec's **antics**.

Brooke had the nerve to say to me, "Can you let me see more of the test?"

I looked over at her, put both of my hands on my hips, and said, "No. I shouldn't have helped you in the first place. And stop telling everybody I was going to help you anyway. You should've studied."

She frowned and looked around. "Well, no one will even notice now. Let me see."

"No, Brooke. I'm not gonna help you," I said, as I put my hands over my paper.

"See, I thought you were my friend." Brooke turned away and huffed.

At that point, I couldn't let Alec get in trouble for me. I had to think of something. Yeah, Brooke was mad at me, but so what. I let her see enough to copy some answers—and that was wrong. But if she didn't get what she needed, oh well.

It's like Mom said, I needed a friend who was gonna help me to do what was right. And Brooke made me see that she didn't care if I got in trouble or not. She only cared about herself and that's why she wanted to copy my test.

A few kids got out of control and started standing on chairs. I quickly went to the door and said, "Mrs. Hardy, everybody's actin' crazy! They're all standin' on chairs. If Alec gets in trouble for standin' on his chair, then we all should. Right?"

Mrs. Hardy hurried past me and walked in to see her

class. "Oh, my goodness! You kids have lost your minds."

"I jumped on my chair first, Mrs. Hardy," Trey called from the back of the room. "Not Alec."

Another boy sitting in the back of the room who barely ever talked said, "No! I did it first, Mrs. Hardy."

"I don't know what game you're trying to play, but it looks like you all are trying to protect your friend. And Alec acted out because he was trying to protect someone else," she said, looking at me. It was like she knew what we were up to.

"Since the whole class is to blame and no one will tell the truth, then no one will have recess tomorrow. Alec, come on back in and take your seat. Everyone, settle down and pass your tests to the front," said Mrs. Hardy. The class did as we were told.

Well, everyone except Brooke. She kept her paper. I could see she still had two rows with no answers. Mrs. Hardy came up to her and held out her hand for it. Brooke looked as if she already knew she had failed.

Mrs. Hardy placed the tests on her desk and walked up to the board. "Now we will talk about facts and opinions. You will need to know this for the standard test. Some statements are facts and some are opinions. Facts are true and opinions represent your thoughts and feelings. For example, 'I saw Alec standing on the desk.' Is that a fact or an opinion?"

Alec raised his hand. "That's a fact, Mrs. Hardy."

"Well, thank you for admitting it. I should have sent

you to the office for that antic. Now, someone else tell me. Is this sentence a fact or an opinion: 'I should have sent you to the office for that antic'?"

"It's your opinion," said Trey, forgetting to raise his hand before he was called on.

"Trey, you did not raise your hand first."

"Sorry, Mrs. Hardy."

"Tell me why you think the sentence is an opinion."

"Because I don't think Alec should have been sent to the office for that. And it seems like you didn't either, since you didn't send him to the office." Then Trey slapped hands with his buddy Alec.

Mrs. Hardy said, "All right, settle down. Next sentence, 'It's hot outside.' It that a fact or an opinion?"

"It's an opinion," someone called out.

"That's correct, but please raise your hand so you'll be recognized," Mrs. Hardy said, looking to see who said it. "Why is it an opinion?"

I raised my hand and so did others in the class. She didn't call on me. She called on Billy.

"Billy, why is it an opinion?"

Billy said, "I might think it's cold or nippy. That's a word my mom says when it's freezing outside."

Then Mrs. Hardy wrote a few more sentences on the board. She called on some students to come up and write "fact" or "opinion" next to them:

Ice cream tastes good. OPINION

The flavor of the ice cream is strawberry. FACT

Everyone should eat ice cream. OPINION

Last Saturday I ate ice cream. FACT

Brooke leaned over to me and said, "We gotta talk because you're not actin' like my best friend. I need you to help me a little more than you were just helping me."

I guess I surprised her because I looked back at her and said, "If you're my best friend, then you need to help yourself. I was about to get in trouble because of you. And you didn't even care."

"But you didn't get in trouble, did you?" She rolled her eyes and looked away.

Oh, no she didn't, I thought! I was hot! I did help her and she wasn't even **grateful**. I wasn't about to do it again.

● ● ● ● ●

I was so happy when school was over. It had been such a long day and I was really tired. All I wanted to do was to sit down on the bus and close my eyes for a few minutes. I knew when I got home I'd have to open them and study some more. But as soon as I got to a seat and tried to sit down, someone pushed me out of the way and sat down before me.

"I can't believe you did that! I was about to sit there," I said to the boy. It was Alec's older brother, Antoine.

The bigger, taller, meaner kid said, "Whatever. You snooze, you lose. You were movin' too slow."

"Excuse me," Alec said from behind me.

I moved aside to let Alec go around me. He grabbed his

brother by the shirt and tried to rough him up. It looked so funny because Antoine was much bigger than his brother. But Alec was mad.

"Why would you do that, man? You saw she was about to sit there. Move!"

"Oh, my bad. You wanna sit there with her?" said Antoine. He laughed as he pushed his brother's hand away from his dirty white shirt.

"Just go to the back. And here, take your stuff with you," Alec said, tossing Antoine his book bag.

Our bus wasn't so full. Pretty much everybody got to have their own seat. Alec sat down right behind me and the bus driver took off. I was really confused. What had gotten into this boy all of a sudden?

I thought, *Lord, why is Alec being so nice to me? He told me I looked pretty on my birthday. He saved me from falling after Billy's sister, Bridget, tripped me. He protected me from getting caught by being a* **diversion** *for Mrs. Hardy. And now he stands up for me with his big brother. Why?*

So I turned around to Alec and said, "Can I ask you something?"

"Yeah, go ahead," he said, as he looked up from the book he was reading.

He said it so cold, though. Not cold like he didn't have any feelings but cold but because he didn't feel like carrying on a conversation. Maybe he was tired like I was and just wanted to rest and read. I decided to ask him another time.

"Never mind," I said, sensing that he didn't wanna talk.

"What? Ask me," he said.

"Okay, but I need you to tell me the truth."

This time in a stronger tone, he said, "Ask me."

Finally getting the words out, I said, "Why are you being so nice to me?"

Alec just looked out the window. I didn't know if he didn't plan on answering my question or if he was just thinking. But I didn't want to ask the question again because I was sure he heard me.

He finally turned to me and said, "I think I told you this before. You were nice to me when no one else was."

"Oh."

"A lot of good changes have happened in my family and I have you to thank for being a part of that. It was pretty rough for a while. If your dad hadn't prayed with my dad, I don't know what we were gonna do. I guess the reason I'm being nice to you is because I think you're cool."

"You do?"

"But being real with you, sometimes you do dumb stuff."

"Excuse me?" I was offended.

"I'm serious. You were about to get in trouble for letting Brooke copy off of your paper. Then the way she acted the rest of day was like she didn't care at all what you **sacrificed**. My mom always says, with friends like that, you don't need enemies."

"Yeah, Brooke and I have a lot to work on. I guess I'm mad at her and she's mad at me. But it'll be okay. Keepin' it real with you, though, I'm still a little surprised that you care about me."

"It's the whole God thing too. It's like you're a kid but you know there's a God up there. That makes you try to do the right things and I wanna be like that. Last year I was being a real mean guy to everybody like there was no God in me. I want to be closer to God like you are, Morgan. Maybe sometimes I can even go to church with your family. I want you to know that I care about you as a friend and I've got your back."

I was really surprised to hear Alec talk that way. As we were about to get off the bus, I said, "We can grow together, Alec. We'll work on it all, schoolwork and God's work—one day at a time."

• • • • •

Another week had gone by and I was disappointed that Brooke and I hadn't worked things out. I cared about her, so I prayed for her. If we were supposed to be friends, then it would just happen. I wasn't going to push it. I had faith.

I did wanna make sure I came to school for the right reasons. Not to hang out with my friends and have a bunch of fun, but to learn. I had to pass the standard test before the end of the third grade year. Anything that Mrs. Hardy wanted to teach me, I was ready to get.

"Okay class, today we will be learning about the three

branches of our country's government. Take out your social studies books and turn to page forty-five. Will someone read the first paragraph for me?"

I raised my hand.

"Morgan, go ahead, dear."

"In 1787, leaders of the states gathered together to write principles that **dictated** how our new nation would be governed. The leaders of the states wanted a strong, national government. However, they also needed to make sure everyone's freedoms were protected and that no one could abuse the powers. So they came up with three branches of government: judicial, legislative, and executive. In the first three articles of the Constitution, this separation is described."

"Very good. So there are three branches of government, class. Now, who is the head of our executive branch? Who can tell me?"

"The president?" Trey said, after being called on.

"That's correct, Trey. The president is head of the executive branch. He is elected by voters throughout the country and he serves a term of four years."

Trey was waving his hand up high. Mrs. Hardy wanted to go on, but she couldn't because his hand was all over the place.

"Yes, Trey?"

"Mrs. Hardy, I wanna be president."

"Well, that's good and someday you may even be elected president of the United States. Soon we'll begin preparing for an upcoming school-wide election. You see, to keep order in the way the school operates and to teach students about how government works, each grade level will elect officers to run the student government. Upper grade students will become president and vice president. And this class will elect someone to represent our third grade class on the student council. The elections will take place in a few weeks and maybe you will want to run."

"Run? I don't wanna run track."

"Well, in this case, the word means that you campaign and run for an office. That means you have to tell the class why you should get the job. But we'll talk more about that later."

Mrs. Hardy continued our lesson on government.

"Next, we have the legislative branch which is made up of the Congress: the House of Representatives and the Senate."

Brooke raised her hand. "I don't understand. The who?"

"I'm going to explain. The House of Representatives is made up of 435 members that represent the people of each state. The Senate is made up of 100 members—two from each state. So tell me, class, what are the two branches that we have gone over so far?"

We all said together, "The executive branch and the legislative branch!"

"Very good. The last branch we have is the judicial branch. This branch is over all the courts in the United

States of America. The justices are known as the Supreme Court. The president nominates justices and the Senate has to approve them. Most important, the decisions made by the justices on the Supreme Court are final. No other court can overrule them."

Trey's hand was going again.

"Wow. They've got a lot of power. Okay, so we have the three branches of government. When I grow up, I might wanna be president or a judge. But right now, what office can I run for?"

Mrs. Hardy went over to her desk and got a letter. "Here is the information. We need a class representative for our student council. I would like for at least two of you all to run so we can have a campaign and then vote. You can nominate; that is, volunteer yourself to run or someone else can nominate you. We will vote just before Thanksgiving and the person who gets the most votes will start in January."

Trey's hand shot straight into the air. "I nominate Trey Spencer! You know, that's me. And I can be your class president because—"

"No, Trey, we are not campaigning right now. And remember, the job will be student representative, not class president. So we don't need to hear why you would make a good **candidate** at this moment. Let me write your name down on the board. Does anyone else want to nominate yourself?"

This was interesting. Maybe I could run too. I mean, I

am a nice person. I care about people. But at the moment, I was too **timid** to nominate myself. Yeah, Trey should have it. He's knows how to speak up. He's not shy at all.

Then Alec raised his hand and Mrs. Hardy called on him. "I nominate Morgan Love."

"Please," Trey said. "She's a girl and you know I'm gonna beat her."

"And I'll help you beat her," Brooke said to Trey, as she looked me in the eye with a cold stare. I looked back at her and could feel no warmth.

Letter to Dad

Dear Dad,

Today I made a bad decision. I helped my friend cheat. I didn't get caught because of my other friend's antics to make the teacher look somewhere else. I was spared and very grateful for the diversion. I know it was wrong, but my girlfriend practically dictated that I help her or we wouldn't be friends anymore.

Dad, I sacrificed by getting in trouble to help her out. But she was still mad at me because I didn't let her copy my whole paper. I won't do it again, though. I promise. I know I keep saying I'll do better, but I will.

Also, I am a candidate for student council representative. I have to run against a popular boy in my class even though I'm timid. I'll keep you posted. Miss you so much, Dad.

> Your daughter,
> Getting it together, Morgan

Word Search

```
X  C  A  N  D  I  D  H  S  O  R  E
D  B  E  P  D  I  C  T  A  T  E  D
I  J  S  C  H  O  O  G  C  I  M  A
C  G  G  A  N  S  L  R  R  M  O  N
T  R  R  N  C  B  P  A  I  E  R  O
A  E  A  D  O  R  M  T  F  D  G  I
N  A  T  I  D  Y  I  E  Y  W  A  S
T  T  E  D  I  N  Q  F  J  K  N  R
I  R  B  A  V  O  R  U  I  D  M  E
C  E  W  T  E  E  W  L  N  C  H  V
S  Y  K  E  R  L  N  A  V  Y  E  I
A  L  E  C  S  L  E  T  I  M  I  D
```

ANTICS

CANDIDATE

DICTATED

DIVERSION

GRATEFUL

SACRIFICED

TIMID

Words to Know and Learn

1) an·tics (ăn'tĭx) *noun*
Playful or funny actions.

2) grate·ful (grāt'fəl) *adjective*
Thankful; appreciative.

3) di·ver·sion (dĭ-vûr'zhən, -shən, dī-) *noun*
Something that draws the attention away from something or someone else.

4) dic·tate (dĭk'tāt', dĭk-tāt'-) *verb* **dic·tat·ed** (past tense)
To say or order with authority.

5) sac·ri·fice (săk'rə-fīs') *verb* **sac·ri·ficed** (past tense)
To give away or allow to be taken away.

6) can·di·date (kăn'dĭ-dāt', -dĭt) *noun*
A person who seeks or is nominated for an office or honor.

7) tim·id (tĭm'ĭd) *adjective*
Fearful and hesitant.

Chapter 4

Always Trouble

It was the morning of the first big field trip. The third grade class was going to the Fernbank Museum of Natural History. It's an exciting museum that teaches about science and allows people to do hands-on exploring and playing.

All everybody kept talking about was bringing their iPods and I had one too. I just needed Mom to say, "Yeah, Morgan you can take yours." I wanted to be enjoying myself and listening to my music on the bus along with everyone else. But that wasn't going to happen.

After I finished getting dressed, I raced to the kitchen to find Mom cooking breakfast. I had to put my best face on because I wanted something so bad. She couldn't dare resist my angel smile. But mommies always know when you're up to something. Always.

"Hey, Mom. You didn't have to fix me this much breakfast. I could have made oatmeal today."

"It's okay, baby. Today is a special day and I wanted to make a special meal to go with your special shirt."

"Thanks for the shirt, Mommy. I love it!" I said, as I twirled around showing off my yellow shirt with its bright pink heart. I was also wearing some cute new skinny leg jeans to match. Then I hugged her really tight.

"Okay, why are you hanging around me all of a sudden, Morgan? What do you want, girl?"

I was caught! She knew me too well.

She added, "I know you want to go to the gift shop. Mrs. Hardy already wrote us a letter and said it was okay if we allowed you to bring a few dollars just in case you wanted to buy some **souvenirs**. So, don't worry, you'll have a few dollars."

Stepping away from her, I looked real sad and responded in a not-so-grateful tone, "Thanks."

"Well, what is it now, girl? You all are going to be served lunch at the museum, so I know you don't need to take food. What's going on?"

Mom stopped mixing the batter of the pancakes and turned my head toward her to look into my eyes. I was thinking about what I wanted to say to her. I mean, I know what I wanted to say. I just didn't know how to say it.

So I started, "Well, all my classmates—"

Cutting me off she said, "Now, you know I don't care about what all of your classmates are doing, so you might as well just end it right there. That's not going to help me do whatever it is you want me to do, which I'm probably going to say no to anyway. It must be something pretty serious for you to hesitate before getting your point across."

"Mom! Please say yes! It's not that bad."

"Tell me. I'm trying to hurry and finish breakfast."

"I got this from my teacher," I said, pulling a note from my pocket and unfolding it so I could hand it to her.

"You have a note from your teacher and I'm just now seeing it? It better not say you have a bad grade because you'll be staying home with me today."

"Mom! You know it's not that."

Reading the note, she said, "Electronics? What electronics, Morgan?"

"My iPod."

"Morgan, do you remember when you were in the first grade?"

"Yes, Mom, I remember. I left my music player at the zoo somewhere and you had to buy me another one."

"Then you also remember me saying that I wasn't going to allow you to take it to school again. I don't want it to end up broken, missing, or stolen. Those things cost too much for me to let you take it to school."

"But—"

"But nothing. Go wash your face, sweetheart, and get ready to eat."

I couldn't believe she said no. My mind wouldn't allow me to hear what she was saying. There was no way I was going to be the only kid on the bus without my iPod. I had to do something. I had to. But, just what was there to do?

I sat at the table looking at Mom with my best puppy dog eyes.

"Don't even try it. The answer is not changing. It's still no."

Because Mom took the time to make me pancakes for breakfast, I missed the bus and she had to take me to school. When Mom was ready to go, I knew it was wrong, but I put my iPod in the front of my book bag and zipped it up. She wouldn't know a thing. I was going to school with it and I would bring it back home with me. I promise.

As we were riding along, I was quiet and just staring out the window.

"Morgan, I know you're a little upset, but I have my reasons why I don't want you taking your iPod to school."

I didn't respond.

"I'm talking to you, young lady. You can be as mad as you want to be with me, but you're going to respect me."

I didn't really wanna say everything was okay. She knew I would be upset because I couldn't take my music. So I couldn't just be quiet. I had to say something.

"Yes, ma'am."

"As you grow older, you'll learn to take better care of your things. Then it won't be an issue."

"Yes, ma'am."

"Right now, I know what's best. Have a good day, sweetie."

As soon as I got out of the car, I ran into Brooke on the way to class.

"Hey, girl."

I couldn't believe Brooke was speaking to me. I had made some new friends in the class and so had she, but I wasn't going to be rude.

"Hey," I replied.

Surprising me even more, she said, "I miss you, Morgan. We're going on the field trip today and I want us to be partners . . . if that's cool with you."

"Brooke, I can't be fake with you."

"I know. I'm sorry. Even though I think best friends should always help each other, when you weren't okay with doing it, I shouldn't have gotten mad with you."

"We could have gotten in trouble, you know?"

"Yeah. But no one is perfect, Morgan. Haven't you ever done anything you weren't so proud of?"

In my mind, I was thinking, *Yeah. I have my iPod in my book bag right now and my mom just told me not to bring it.*

I didn't even respond to Brooke. I walked right into the classroom. Not too soon after I stepped in the door, Mrs. Hardy asked everyone who had an electronic device to show their notes. Everybody had a note except for me!

I was stumbling over my words. "I—I—"

"We came in together this morning, Mrs. Hardy, and the wind was blowing so hard it just blew hers away," Brooke said, without even blinking. The fib she told felt so real even I believed it.

"Yeah, my note was flying in the air." I joined in and added to the story.

"And you saw it, Brooke?"

Brooke said with confidence, "Yes, ma'am. It flew away like a bird. She couldn't even catch it."

"Well then, sit down girls," Mrs. Hardy said to us before speaking to the class.

"As soon as the morning announcements are over, class, it'll be time to line up and go straight to the buses."

"Your Mom didn't give you a note, did she?" Brooke asked. I just looked at her and sat down at my desk.

"See, friends are always supposed to have each other's back. Just make sure you don't lose the thing so your mom won't find out and the teacher won't find out that we made up the note story. We don't want to get in trouble."

I just put my head on my desk. I knew I was in some mess now. Brooke was talking like I owed her.

• • • • •

On the way to the museum, the class was having so much fun. Some people were talking. Some people were laughing. Everybody else was listening to their iPods. Although I had worked it so I could have mine with me, I just couldn't pull it out. I didn't even wanna play it. I knew it was wrong and I wished I hadn't brought it. If I had a cell phone, I would have taken it out right then and called my mom to tell her I'm sorry.

I remember when I got in trouble for watching the PG-

13 movie she told me not to watch the night Brooke stayed over. My mom told me that all I have is my word and that she needed to be able to trust me to always be honest.

I can honestly say watching the movie was not my idea. But taking the iPod when I wasn't supposed to have brought it was nobody's fault but my own. Instead of Brooke pointing out that I was wrong for that, she was right there and ready to carry out a fib to help me. Neither of us was being a good example for each another. I felt sick.

When we stepped off the bus, Alec came up beside me and said, "You're changing."

I just looked at him and rolled my eyes. I didn't know what he was talking about, and I didn't have time for anyone to make me feel worse. I huffed and turned away from him.

He came up behind me again and said, "Don't get mad at me. I'm just stating a fact."

"What are you talking about, Alec?" I said, feeling a pain in my stomach.

"I saw your mom drop you off and I saw you hook up with Brooke. No paper flew away that I could see. Plus, you didn't even sound **convincing** when you gave that lame excuse to the teacher. So even if I didn't see you walking into school with my own eyes, I wouldn't have believed you. To be honest, I don't think Mrs. Hardy believes you either."

I looked around to find my teacher and she was looking straight at me. She had two fingers on her chin like she was **pondering** what to say. Or maybe I was totally mis-reading her because Alec had made me fearful.

"You don't know what you're talkin' about, Alec. Are you sayin' that I'm not telling the truth about the note? What difference does it make to you anyway? It's my life."

"Yeah, but that's why I say you're changing. I thought it was cool the way you love God. But how can you be honest when you made up the story about a note? Your mom probably told you not to bring that thing. And you were feeling so guilty about it you didn't even wanna listen to it on the bus."

He was so right about it. So I asked him, "Why are you watching me so hard? How come you know everything I'm doing?"

"Forget it. I'm just tryin' to help you out." Without saying another word, he walked away.

I felt dizzy. This lying stuff was too much. I had to get myself together. I didn't need anybody helping me out. My **conscience** was already telling me that I was wrong. Mrs. Hardy started walking over to me. I didn't know what she was going to say so all I could think to do was smile. And even that was hard to do.

"Morgan, are you okay?" she asked. "I saw you holding your stomach. Do I need to call your mom? Are you sick?"

"I'm okay."

"Very well. Class, it's time for us to go inside," Mrs. Hardy said, as she walked away from me and headed to the front of the line.

Then I realized that she was watching me because she thought I might be sick. But I was sick of being fake and phony. I just wasn't sick enough to go home. That's when I made up my mine to enjoy my field trip and not think about all this stuff anymore.

Brooke came and put her arm around my shoulders. "I'm glad we're friends again. See, you're not such a good girl. We're pretty much the same. You're a little bad, too," she said, smiling and squeezing my arm.

"I already feel awful, Brooke. Don't make it worse."

"Come on. Let's just check out the science museum. Relax."

The dinosaur exhibit was **phenomenal**. There was a life-size dinosaur and it was huge! We watched a short video that re-created what it was like before people lived on the earth. During that time, there were meat-eating dinosaurs and plant-eating dinosaurs. The meat-eating ones were mean looking like the T. rex.

Then we went to check out the fossils. There were a ton of bones from different places and **artifacts** from different cultures. My favorite one was a very old wedding headpiece. It was made from big, pretty rocks and it stood higher than the Miss America crown I saw when I watched that program last year.

Brooke liked the last exhibit. It was hands-on and you could use all your senses to make it work. The five senses are seeing, hearing, touching, smelling, and tasting.

It was a fun day full of exploring and learning about how

cool science is. I really wasn't a fan of science until I spent time in the woods this past summer. It had felt good to have the wind blowing on my face. I got to see a lot of birds and hear the different sounds of their chirping. Most of all, being outside and enjoying nature made me feel closer to God.

It was time to board the bus to go back to school. Just then I was reminded that I had disrespected my mom and didn't tell my teacher the truth. It was the wrong thing to do and I was feeling really down as I stepped on the bus to take a seat. When I put my book bag down, Brooke grabbed it right away and pulled out my iPod. She started dancing around and acting silly.

"What are you doing? Give that back," I said, trying to yank it from her.

"I wanna hear the songs that I might not have on mine. What's the big deal?"

"I don't want to have it out, okay?"

Brooke huffed. "Fine."

She snatched it out of her ears and threw it at me. She didn't understand how bad I felt. And she didn't care. I stuffed it back in the front pocket of my book bag. I just wanted to get it home in one piece and put this bad situation behind me.

● ● ● ● ●

"Morgan Love, I want to speak to you," Mrs. Hardy said to me when we got back to school. She allowed the rest of the class to go on into the classroom.

"Yes, ma'am?" I said to her when we were alone in the hallway. "I feel better, Mrs. Hardy."

"I don't know if you're going to feel okay as soon as I tell you what I have to say."

All of a sudden, I felt a lump in my throat. Oh, my goodness, she knew! She knew I had my iPod and I wasn't supposed to. I was so in trouble. But maybe I was glad too because it was a lot of work keeping up with a fib.

"You spoke to my mom and she told you about the note. Right? I'm so sorry, Mrs. Hardy, I didn't tell you the truth. It won't happen again. I felt so bad that I didn't even play it on the bus. But I am an honest person. I just had one episode of weakness."

"Let me stop you right there, young lady. 'Episode of weakness'? I don't even know where you got that from."

"From a TV show. It sounds smart, right?"

"Let's start from the top. You told me a completely different story this morning. And because you are a good student I trusted you. As strange as it sounded, I believed it. That was my fault. Since it kept bothering me, I wanted to give you another chance before I call your mom. So I'm glad you told me the truth. I still have to follow this up with your mother."

My eyes began to tear faster than if Mrs. Hardy had pushed the button on the water fountain and the water sprang up. The tears fell but they were silent. I wasn't boohoo crying on the outside. I was just feeling awful inside. What was I going to do? Still I hoped it was the right thing to do by finally telling her the truth. But, no doubt about it, I was in real trouble now.

"Go on to the washroom, Morgan, and dry your eyes. Then we'll call your mother. She may come and pick you up so you don't have to ride the bus. We need to talk about this."

I just nodded my head.

"Here, take your book bag with you. The bell's about to ring and kids will be all over this hallway. I'll be in the classroom when you come out."

I walked into the washroom and put my book bag on the floor next to the sink. I couldn't believe I'd put my foot in my mouth! I told on myself and got myself in trouble. Why didn't I just wait and let Mrs. Hardy say what she had to say? I had made such a mess. Now I was really in for it.

As soon as I went into the stall, I heard the bathroom door open and two girls come in. They started giggling. "Did you see her come in here?" one of them asked.

"Look, there's her book bag right there and the cord is hanging out the side. It's easy to grab."

I wasn't sure, but I thought that I'd heard one of the voices before when she said, "Well, come on, let's steal it before she finds out."

"Wait! Steal it?" the other girl asked.

"Yeah, steal it."

I heard some scrambling. They were going through my things! As much as I wanted to, I couldn't get out the stall quick enough.

"Who's there?" I said.

Then the bathroom lights were flicked off and I got scared. I was breathing so hard I could pass out. I had to hurry so I could stop them.

"We got it. Let's go!"

Finally, I was all buttoned up. I ran out of the stall and tripped over my book bag. My vision must have been **blurry**. They'd placed it in the center of the floor. I fell forward and hit my head hard on the sink.

Feeling worse than ever, I prayed, *Lord, I feel really weak and my head hurts really bad. I can't get up. I think those girls stole my iPod that I wasn't even supposed to have at school. Help me, Lord. Please.*

I just lay there in the dark, hurting. I don't know how long it was, but the next thing I knew, the lights came on. And I could hear a voice calling out to me.

"Morgan, are you in here? Mrs. Hardy sent me to—" Brooke started. "Oh, my goodness! What happened? There's a ton of blood! Don't worry, Morgan, I'll go and get help!"

"Blood?" I said.

I have got to start doing the right things. When I don't—there's always trouble.

Letter to Dad

Dear Dad,

Today my class went on a field trip to the natural history museum. I got you and baby Jayden a couple of cool **souvenirs**. The museum has some interesting and **convincing** exhibits. One of them made us feel like we were living in the dinosaur age. As I was **pondering** the thought of living with those large animals, it made me happy to be living right now.

Dad, I must tell you the truth. I made another mistake and my **conscience** has gotten the best of me. Mom is **phenomenal** and I let her down. I took my iPod to school after she told me not to. You may only find my **artifacts** when you come home because I'm really in trouble. I can't even say my vision was **blurry** and I wasn't thinking straight. I don't know why I did it. But it didn't pay off. I know you're disappointed.

Your daughter,
Bad decision maker, Morgan

Word Search

```
K  B  C  R  E  A  M  W  H  S  X  C
E  T  L  I  S  U  G  A  R  R  S  O
P  C  N  U  T  C  R  C  S  I  O  N
O  H  N  F  R  O  S  O  T  N  N  V
N  U  E  K  H  R  U  N  C  E  N  I
D  P  E  N  M  N  Y  S  A  V  Y  N
E  N  M  E  O  E  V  C  F  U  B  C
R  I  U  W  B  M  N  I  I  O  H  I
I  G  S  C  E  R  E  E  T  S  E  N
N  H  T  A  R  D  Y  N  R  Z  R  G
G  T  O  W  D  T  S  C  A  R  P  T
K  N  I  G  H  T  V  E  N  L  Y  R
```

ARTIFACTS

BLURRY

CONSCIENCE

CONVINCING

PHENOMENAL

PONDERING

SOUVENIRS

Words to Know and Learn

1) sou·ve·nir (sū'və-nîr', sū'və-nîr') *noun*
A token of remembrance; a memento.

2) con·vinc·ing (kən-vĭn'sĭng) *adjective*
Believable.

3) pon·der (pŏn'dər) *verb* **pon·der·ing**
Thinking about carefully.

4) con·science (kŏn'shəns) *noun*
A sense of right and wrong.

5) phe·nom·e·nal (fĭ-nŏm'ə-nəl) *adjective*
Something that is extraordinary or outstanding.

6) ar·ti·fact (är'tə-făkt') *noun*
An object produced or shaped by human craft, especially a tool, weapon, or ornament of archaeological or historical interest.

7) blur·ry (blûr"rў) *adjective*
Blurred or not distinct.

Chapter 5

Pretty Awesome

I was so glad Brooke went to get help, but I was frightened that I wouldn't be okay. My head was hurting so bad. I could see red liquid all around me even though I was in a daze. So I tried to take some deep breaths and stay calm because seeing the blood was scary. When I thought about what Jesus would do, I knew I had to pray.

Lord, help me not to be hurt too badly. I can't even get up and I know that's not good. Please send someone to help me soon. Please.

Before I could even say Amen, I heard the voice of my teacher from last year. Miss Nelson pushed open the door.

"I heard a lot of noise in here. Somebody just came running out of this washroom. Who's in here? What's going—?"

Seeing me lying on the floor, she called out, "Morgan, oh, my goodness! What happened?"

I groaned. Then the sweet smell of her perfume lightly touched across my nose. She lifted my head and held me close. It was enough to make my fast breathing slow down.

"It hurts," I sighed, trying to lift my hand up to my forehead but Miss Nelson held on to it.

"Don't move, Morgan. I'm going to go and get some help."

"No, don't go." I was weak and it was hard to get the words out. "Stay with me, please."

Just then, we heard Brooke yell, "She's in here! Hurry!"

Mrs. Hardy came rushing in. "Oh, my goodness, Morgan! This is terrible!"

"I know. I just found her like this," said Miss Nelson.

"I sent Brooke in here to check on her and then she came back in a panic saying Morgan was hurt. What in the world happened? Let me go up to the front office. Please stay here with her."

A few more teachers came in and so did the school nurse. They carried me to her office and laid me on the small bed. I was going in and out . . . really tired . . . in a lot of pain. In my dizzy state, I could still see a bunch of adults in front of me, trying to help me be okay.

The principal, Dr. Sharpe, came. "Her mom has been contacted. She's on the way."

"Oh, no. She's gonna be so mad at me. I have to get out of here," I said, trying to get up.

"No, you can't, Morgan. You've been hurt pretty bad and we need you to take it easy," Miss Nelson said to me.

I was **ecstatic** that she was here by my side. I guess an assistant teacher was watching her class while she was away. She made it clear that she wasn't leaving me and I loved her for that. Miss Nelson was the best. Though Mrs. Hardy was tougher, she seemed worried too. It was good to know people cared.

"Morgan, sweetie, I need you to talk to us and tell us what you remember. Dr. Sharpe is reviewing the security tape in the hall. It must have been some wrong conduct that caused this."

"Yes," Miss Nelson said. "I heard a lot of noise going on in the washroom and I went in to check. Thank goodness, I did. You're going to be okay, Morgan."

Miss Nelson was giving me care, and Mrs. Hardy was getting right down to the business of finding out what happened.

"If someone did this to you, Morgan, you need to tell us what you know so we can take care of this matter."

"I remember somebody was trying to take my iPod and I wanted to stop them. You see, I wasn't supposed to have it in the first place. When my mom finds out, she's gonna be mad at me. Oh, no! What am I gonna do?" I was so shaken up, I couldn't even finish my thoughts.

"Calm down, Morgan," said Dr. Sharpe as she entered the room. "We'll talk to your mom about that. Right now we need to understand everything that happened. We have to get to the bottom of this."

"I heard some girls laughing and then the lights went

off. I was in the washroom stall. As soon as I got myself together, I walked out and tripped over my book bag. It was dark and I hit my head on the sink I guess. It hurt really bad."

"We'll be able to determine who went into the bathroom around the same time you did. You can't remember who the girls were in there with you?"

"No, ma'am. The only other person I saw was Brooke. Mrs. Hardy sent her to come and check on me. I did hear two more voices and one of them sounded familiar, but I don't know who it was."

Dr. Sharpe stated, "Okay, we can get to the bottom of this. I told the students at the beginning of the year that our discipline policy is firm. We have cameras that monitor all hallway activity and we record the whole time school is in session. Some students don't understand that we are serious. I'm going to make an example out of this."

"So, no one pushed you?" Mrs. Hardy asked, double checking.

"No, ma'am, I tripped because it was dark."

Miss Nelson said, "But if the lights hadn't been turned off, then you wouldn't have tripped. Right?"

"Yes, ma'am. That's cause and effect."

She laughed. "That's right, sweetie. That's cause and effect."

"And I know my mom is gonna say if I hadn't brought my iPod, none of this would have happened. I'm gonna be in big trouble," I said, squeezing her hand.

"Maybe so. But just because you did something you weren't supposed to doesn't make it right for someone else to do something wrong. We're going to fix this."

The teachers all loved us kids so much. When they took the time to explain why rules are important and why we must obey them, it made me feel good. The talk I was hearing now didn't make my head feel any better, though.

● ● ● ● ●

"Oh, my goodness! Oh, my goodness!" Mom shouted, seeing the nurse and the teachers standing over me with a bloody **compress** on my head.

"Thanks for getting here so quickly, Mrs. Randall," Dr. Sharpe said to my mom. "We are checking into the situation and Morgan is still telling us what happened. It turns out that some girls went into her book bag and stole her iPod."

I was waiting on my mom to start flipping out and say, *See, Morgan, this is exactly what you get. I told you not to bring that thing to school and you did it anyway! This is what happens when you disobey your mother's wishes.*

But instead she just rushed over to me and hugged me. I loved her so much at that moment. I was wrong but she was giving me grace. I knew I would have to take it if she had let me have it, but right now being in her arms felt so safe. Her touch felt so good that it made some of the pain go away.

"Come on, sweetie. We need to get you to the hospital."

"But I thought they said I was gonna be okay," I asked, not wanting to go to that scary place.

The nurse said, "You are, but you may need stitches. And just in case, they'll want to take some X-rays to make sure there are no other problems. Okay?"

Now I was even more afraid. I had been to the hospital before. Not for me but to visit other people. I went to see Mom when she had the baby. I saw Billy when he got struck by lightning. And all of those needles weren't something I wanted to be around at all.

I listened closely as Dr. Sharpe went on to tell my mom the details about how they were looking into things for me.

"When we find out more information, Mrs. Randall, we will let you know right away."

As soon as we got into the car and my mom made sure I was comfortable, I said to Mom, "How come the principal wouldn't just let us go? She kept saying what they were gonna do over and over."

"Dr. Sharpe just wanted to make sure that she protected herself and that the school took care of my baby properly. It can be a **liability** if they don't act on things in a certain way."

"A liability? I don't understand."

"Morgan, just relax, sweetie. A liability means something that can get them in trouble. But I'm not concerned with any of that. I'm just worried about making sure you're okay."

"I know, Mom, but don't drive so fast," I said, as I

watched the car going too close to the curb.

Mom took a deep breath. "I know, you're right." Then she prayed, "Lord, thank You for letting my baby be okay."

It had been a while since I heard her pray out loud. But I remember when I was little and she would do it all the time. *Lord, help me pay the bills. Lord, help us be okay. Lord, please continue to bless my baby girl.* Her talking to the Lord that way made me feel a lot better.

"Mom, I'm okay," I said, as I saw the worry on her face.

"I know, Morgan. But the school's already called the emergency room and they're waiting for us."

"But, Mom, I don't want to go to the hospital."

"They're going to take good care of you, Morgan. It'll be okay."

An hour later, I found out I had to get stitches. They **numbed** an area on my forehead with a little needle. As the nice doctor talked to me, he asked me to count from 0 to 100. By the time I got to 50, I had three stitches.

The tests that Mom said they had to run went fine. They told Mom I would have to rest for two days before going back to school. She had to make sure I did no more harm to my head. It was still hurting. What a lesson I'd learned.

When we finally got back in the car, I said, "I'm sorry, Mom."

"Talk to me, baby. What's going on?"

"I took the iPod when you told me not to. This is what I get."

"Morgan, don't say that. Yes, there are consequences to sin. Disobeying me and going against my wishes is definitely a sin. The Bible says to honor your mother and father. It's one of the Ten **Commandments** and it means do what I say. But you didn't. So, yes, there is trouble. But no one wanted this for you. Punishment maybe . . .

"I do want you to understand that when you do something wrong, a lot of trouble can come from your bad actions. Thank you for saying you're sorry. I'm glad you see that if you hadn't taken your music player none of this would have happened."

Of course, I knew that she was right and I was listening to every word she said.

"You probably think Mom is trying to spoil your fun by not letting you do stuff other kids get to do. But that's not the case. As your Mom, I know when something isn't good for you. I love you and I want the best for you. When I say no to you, I don't want you to think that it's the end of the world."

"Yes, ma'am," I said, knowing how much she loved me.

"I thought you understood all of this after I caught you watching that movie with Brooke, but I guess not. Now you had to get stitches because you didn't obey me. You're still too young to make some choices and I'm here as your mother to guide you. We're not going to be perfect in this life, Morgan, but we certainly can learn to make better choices each day."

"What do you mean, we're not perfect? I'm going to be perfect from now on," I said, truly believing that.

"You're human, Morgan. You're going to make mistakes. No one is ever going to be perfect until they go to heaven. The only perfect human that walked this earth was our Lord, Jesus Christ. But I hear you. You try to be perfect from now on. For your sake and mine, do the right thing. If we had to go through all of this for you to get that point, it was worth it. You'll be okay."

Then Mom added something extra. "Maybe when you're thirty, we'll get you another iPod."

She laughed. And even with my headache, I laughed too. I loved my mom. She loved me. And she was funny.

●　●　●　●　●

The first day out of school was so cool. Mom didn't have to go to work. She stayed with me and took good care of me. It's not that she wasn't there for me the second day, but she was busy. She was doing her work from home. Mom had **conference** calls to make and lots to do on her computer.

All she wanted me to do was stay in bed and rest. But I was tired of resting. I wanted to learn something. I missed my friends. I didn't want to get behind in my schoolwork. Now that I think about it, I was sorry that I had messed up my perfect attendance too.

When Mom came in and checked on me, she said, "Our neighbor down the street, Alec's father, called and asked if it was okay for Alec to come over and bring your schoolwork. I said that was fine, so go ahead and get dressed. I'll make you both a snack. He'll be here in a little while."

Even though I was home, Mom wouldn't let me watch TV. That was my punishment. She said that it would last for a couple of days. I didn't mind. I was excited about talking to Alec and doing my homework. Sure enough, when the school bus pulled up at our usual spot, I looked out the window and saw him coming straight up to my house.

"Go on in the kitchen, Morgan. I'll get the door."

When she opened it, I heard Mom say, "Well, hello, young man."

"Hello, Mrs. Randall."

"What's all that in your hand?"

"It's something the class made for Morgan."

"Come on in. She's in the kitchen. Your dad says you only have thirty minutes before you have to make it on home, okay?"

"Yes, ma'am."

"There are some snacks on the kitchen table."

"Ooh, thank you," Alec said, ready to eat.

Because I heard my mom say that, I took the brownies off of the kitchen table and hid them from his view. Alec came into the room and didn't even say hi to me. He looked disappointed when he only saw the tall glass of milk.

"This is your mom's idea of a snack?" he said, frowning.

"No," I teased, putting the plate full of chocolate treats in front of him.

"Ooh, your mom is the best. Oh, and these are for you," he said, as he dumped a whole bunch of cards into my lap.

I didn't even have to ask him what they were. The class had made me get-well cards. Some were neat and colorful. Some rhymed. Some just said get well, but all of them were special to me.

"We had a lot of homework too. Mrs. Hardy said that she would give you time to do it, but I thought I'd go ahead and bring it to you so you could get it done. We had some work in Challenge too, but that teacher said she would give it to your mom."

"Thanks, Alec, for bringing my work to me," I said, as I looked through the worksheets. "Oh, my goodness. The 9 facts? We just learned the 7s and 8s a few days ago!"

"Yep, but the 9s are easy."

"Really? How can the 9s be easy?"

"Yeah. Hold out both of your hands," said Alec.

I did what he said and put out my hands.

"If you're gonna say 9x1, you take the thumb on your left hand and put it down. Now how many do you have?"

"Nine," I answered.

"Yep. So 9x1 is 9. Then if you're gonna say 9x2, then you put your second finger down by your thumb. How many do you have by your thumb?"

"One."

"Okay, so that's one in the tens place. And how many fingers are behind the finger that's down?"

"Eight."

"So 8 goes in the ones place."

"Eighteen," I said, getting it.

"Okay. So try the 3."

"Okay. I put my third finger down. That leaves me with a 2 in the tens place and 7 in the ones place. So 9x3 is 27?"

Proud of me, Alec said, "That's right."

It felt good to catch on. I said, "And 4x9 is 36! 5x9 is 45! 6x9 is 54!"

We kept putting our fingers down and it kept working. I was learning something new at home! Now this was cool.

"Of course, you're gonna have to know your other three 9s like from the 10s, 11s, and 12s. But you already know 9x10 is 90. And 9x11 is?"

"Ninety-nine."

"Correct. So all you have to remember from your 9s is 9x12 and that's 108. This is the quick way to learn them, but I thought it was a cool trick. You still have to memorize them for the test."

"Yeah."

"Guess what they found out?"

"What?"

"They know who took your iPod."

"No way! Who?"

"Yep. We've all seen Billy's sister, Bridget, with it. She's a fifth grader and she thinks she runs the school. It's the

same girl who tried to trip you that one time. She was goin'
around braggin' about how she got it and the other girl got
mad at her because she wasn't sharin' it with her. Billy was
tryin' to take up for his sister but she was actin' so **arrogant**. When the principal asked her about it, she had it in
her desk."

"How do you know?"

"You know my brother's in her class," Alec said. Then
his look turned serious. "I'm sorry this happened to you."

"Me too, but it's okay. I learned a lot. You were right,
Alec. I was changin'. You have to do the right thing for
good things to happen to you," I said, being honest.

"So, do you think I should ask your mom if I can take
the rest of these brownies home before I just snatch them
up?" Alec was trying to make me laugh and not feel so bad.

I did laugh. "Go ahead; she made them for you."

"Yes!" he said, as he grabbed a napkin and dashed for
the door.

A part of me felt bad because Billy's sister was in trouble for stealing my iPod. But, as Mom said, sin has consequences. I was reading the Bible more since I'd been home.
I learned more about the Commandments. We are not supposed to steal. I hope Bridget learned a lesson from all of
this too. That way, I guess everything turned out pretty
awesome.

Letter to Dad

Dear Dad,

Well, I think Mom told you that I got hurt badly at school. I know you were **ecstatic** to learn I'm okay. I had a **compress** on my head. All the teachers and the nurse did the right things at school, so they don't have any **liability**. They made sure I was extra okay. I had to get stitches, but I was big girl. I didn't feel it because they **numbed** the area first. YEAH!

Dad, I blame myself for breaking the Commandments. I'm supposed to honor my mother and my father. Mom and I had a **conference**. She told me that when she says no it's not to keep me from having fun but because she knows best. We're really having a better relationship. She listens to me and I promise not to be **arrogant** anymore. I won't do things my way because I'll listen to her too. Love you!

Your daughter,
Stitched up, Morgan

Word Search

```
C  C  E  A  N  T  U  B  T  C  T  R
C  O  J  L  L  N  Y  C  R  O  S  L
S  M  N  M  A  A  U  G  H  M  E  I
P  M  C  F  R  G  A  M  O  P  L  A
G  A  P  A  E  O  F  E  B  R  T  B
H  N  R  Q  U  R  T  O  R  E  P  I
E  D  E  O  K  R  E  B  E  S  D  L
T  M  E  O  K  A  E  N  E  S  D  I
T  E  S  C  N  A  J  N  C  S  P  T
T  N  K  I  X  S  O  S  C  E  P  Y
I  T  C  I  T  A  T  S  C  E  R  Y
F  S  M  E  A  T  B  A  L  L  S  J
```

ARROGANT

COMMANDMENTS

COMPRESS

CONFERENCE

ECSTATIC

LIABILITY

NUMBED

Words to Know and Learn

1) **ec·stat·ic** (ĕk-stăt′ĭk) *adjective*
Showing joy and enthusiasm.

2) **com·press** (kŏm′prĕs′) *noun*
A soft pad of gauze or other material applied with pressure to a part of the body to control bleeding or ease pain.

3) **li·a·bil·i·ty** (lī′ə-bĭl′ĭ-tē) *noun*
Potential for being held responsible.

4) **numb** (nŭm) *verb* **numbed** (past tense)
To cause to not be able to feel.

5) **com·mand·ment** (kə-mănd′mənt) *noun*
God's laws and rules found in the Bible.

6) **con·fer·ence** (kŏn′fər-əns, -frəns) *noun*
A meeting to discuss something.

7) **ar·ro·gant** (ăr′ə-gənt) *adjective*
Overly self-confident or proud.

Chapter 6

Kind Enough

It was my first day back and everyone was so happy to see me. They were clapping and cheering as soon as I stepped in the classroom. I stood up in the front of the room and said, "Thanks so much for the cards, guys. They were really nice. It's good to have friends who care."

Trey raised his hand and was shaking it in the air, as usual. So much so, Mrs. Hardy said, "Go ahead, Trey, if you must."

"We just knew how much you like cards. Remember last year when we made a big card for Tim?"

I smiled wide. I did remember when we made a huge "I'm Sorry" card for Tim, the boy in the special ed class. We had hurt his feelings—especially me. Tim was now our friend. When we pass him in the hall, he high fives us. Tim was always a helper. He pushes some of his classmates around who are in wheelchairs. Now, he's also a leader.

Our actions to make him feel included paid off big time.

Mrs. Hardy spoke up, "Thank you, Trey. Thank you, Morgan; we're glad you're back. Now, we need to get to work. Okay class, moving forward, it's time for us to turn to the subject of English. This lesson will help you prepare for the standard test that's coming up next spring."

Everybody, including me, moaned and groaned. Whenever we heard about that test, it sounded like the end of the world. We had to pass reading and math, and we knew it. It was a must. But Mrs. Hardy made us feel like we were all going to do it. So we got ready for the review.

Getting on us about the moans, Mrs. Hardy warned, "Zip it. I don't want to hear any of that. If you're prepared, you're going to do well on the test. We will go over a few important things here. Let's talk about the main idea of a **passage**. Does anyone know what a main idea is?"

Brooke raised her hand. "Isn't a sentence in a passage?"

"Okay, yes. A passage is made up of sentences. I'm looking for a little bit more."

Alec raised his hand.

"Alec?"

"The main idea, Mrs. Hardy, is the sentence that best describes what the whole paragraph is about."

"Exactly. Now, let's talk about contractions. What is the contraction for the words *I am*?"

Trey raised his hand. "It's I'm. I apostrophe m."

"Very good. What about, *you are*? What is the contraction?"

94

A boy in the back of the classroom next to Trey raised his hand and said, "It's y-o apostrophe u-r-e. Yo'ure."

"Close, but not quite."

Then Brooke raised her hand.

"Yes, Brooke?"

"It's y-o-u apostrophe r-e. You're."

"Correct. What about *it is*?"

I raised my hand and answered once I was called on. "I-t apostrophe s. It's."

Feeling satisfied that we understood what they are, Mrs. Hardy said, "I'll give you a list of contractions to take home and practice some more. Now, what's a compound word?"

Trey raised his hand. "It's two words that are put together to make one word."

"Okay. Now give me an example."

"Campground. Camp is a word and ground is a word, but if you put them together, they make one."

"Great. Bookcase. Football. Cupcake. All of those are compound words. Now, turn in your textbooks to page 46. Some of the reading passages are going to look different from others. You will have to determine if each passage is a story, a poem, a letter, or a report. Let's talk about the differences. A story will contain several paragraphs. A poem will be centered with rhyming words. A report can also have paragraphs that give information. But a letter has a **salutation**. What is a salutation of a letter?"

"Dear, or hello, at the top of the page!" someone shouted out.

"That's right, but don't forget to raise your hands, young people. A letter should also have the date it was written and the address of the person who will receive it. Okay, so I'll give you all a few pages of English to work on right now."

Then Mrs. Hardy explained, "An encyclopedia is made up of a number of volumes, which are separate books that are in alphabetical order. I need to know what volume you find the answers in. For example, in what volume would you find the word *apple*?"

I raised my hand. "It would be in volume A."

"And why?"

"Because volume A has all the words that start with *A*."

"Exactly."

All of a sudden, the secretary's voice came over the loudspeaker.

"Mrs. Hardy?"

"Yes?"

"Could you please send Morgan Love to the office?"

"I sure will."

All of my classmates said, "Ooooh!"

Brooke leaned over to me and said, "I bet this has somethin' to do with Billy's sister."

Sure enough, when I reached the front office, Bridget was sitting down and the principal was with her. It reminded me of the whole **scenario** last year when I had to go to the office and tell Tim that I was sorry for hurting him. But this time it was even more serious because the school resource officer, Officer Kraft, was there too. He looked sort of scary, all dressed in his police uniform.

"Morgan, on the day of your accident, you told Dr. Sharpe all that happened. Since then, Bridget has been seen on camera with your music player. And she has told several of her friends that she took your music device."

"But I don't have it right now!" Bridget blurted out. Her eyes were really watery.

"Don't you have something else to say to Morgan?" asked Officer Kraft.

"We were just tryin' to have a little fun." Bridget wasn't even trying to say she was sorry.

I was a little timid. This girl was bigger than me and I had gotten hurt trying to catch up with her. I didn't know what to say to her.

"Well, are you gonna forgive me or what?" she asked with an attitude.

I didn't know if she was really sorry. The way she was asking me to forgive her didn't sound like anybody that was feeling bad. But I thought about what Jesus would do and I had to realize it wasn't about her. Tim had forgiven me last year. My mom had forgiven me for bringing my iPod to school. Now it was time for me to forgive Bridget.

I looked at her and said, "Yes. I forgive you."

"Good. Can I go back to class now?" She looked over at Dr. Sharpe.

"No, Bridget. You wait right here. You're being suspended as of today. Your mom is on her way to pick you up. Morgan, you may head on back to class. I'll walk with you," Dr. Sharpe said, as we headed to the hallway.

"Morgan, I wanted to tell you that I really **appreciate** your heart. You were kind to someone who really didn't deserve it. Her family is going through a lot. Thank you. We hope to get your music player back."

"It's okay."

"You're a good girl, Morgan."

"I'm tryin' to be, ma'am."

• • • • •

My parents were gone somewhere for the weekend and baby Jayden was staying with our cousins Sam, Drake, and Sadie's mom. They wanted me to visit with them too, but knowing I'd be spoiled by Mama and Papa, I chose to stay with them.

We always have fun together. After breakfast, we were going to the mall and to the movies and then out to dinner.

On Saturday morning, I woke up ready to get out of the bed. Mama had the house smelling so good. The smell of French toast and sausages helped me spring to my feet, throw on my robe, and dash to the kitchen.

"Slow down, girl. That food ain't goin' nowhere. Unless Miss May eats it all," Papa whispered to me as he leaned down.

Miss May was my grandparents' next-door neighbor. I just remembered that she was a lady who talked a whole lot. Every time Mama and Papa were ready for her to go, she made a way to keep talking instead. She was sitting at the kitchen table, eating some French toast and looking upset.

"I mean, I told the child I was gonna help her. But I can't keep them at my house for too long. I need my space. I finally got my daughter up and out. Now I gotta take care of my niece and her two kids . . . for goodness' sake."

I wasn't supposed to listen in when adults were talking. I just always thought if they knew I was in the room then they knew I'd hear. It couldn't be my fault if I heard their words.

Mama said, "May, you know you had to take in that child since lightning struck her little boy a while back."

"Yeah, and the medical bills just wiped out all her money. She couldn't even afford to pay the rent for her townhouse. And that sassy older daughter of hers keeps gettin' in trouble. If she steals one more thing from my house, I'm tellin' you . . . " Miss May complained.

Then it dawned on me. An older child who takes things and a boy who got struck by lightning.

"Is Billy at your house?" I said, forgetting the fact that I wasn't supposed to be listening.

"Girl, is anybody talkin' to you?"

Mama responded, "Don't speak to my granddaughter like that, May."

Miss May threw her hands up in the air and said, "I'm just sayin', you know we're havin' grown-up talk."

"I'm sorry, Mama. I just couldn't help hearing."

"That's right. Don't go blaming that baby for nothin'

when y'all saw her walk up in here," Papa said. "That's what's wrong with grown folks. They don't want kids to know everything but they say everything in front of kids."

Miss May got up from her chair and said, "That's my fault, baby. Do you know my Billy?"

"May, you know we all know Billy. You're the one who told the church he got struck by lightning and was in the hospital. We took Morgan over there to see him. Remember?"

"Oh yeah, that's right."

I didn't even realize my grandparents had gotten all of the news about my classmate from their next-door neighbor. She was Billy's aunt. Then again, I was a kid and I didn't know everything. I just listened some more.

"Well, land's sake! Billy told me that the girl who came to see him in the hospital was the one his sister stole somethin' from. Oh, my goodness!" Miss May said. "I'm gonna get that little girl. She just don't know . . . stealing from my best friend's granddaughter . . ."

Quickly, I said, "But it's okay now, Miss May. Bridget said she was sorry and I already forgave her."

"I don't even believe that! I'm givin' them a place to stay. I'm lettin' them eat all of my food. I know that's my niece and I love her, but that little girl hasn't even told me thank you. At least Billy washes the dishes and takes out the trash. Kids these days . . ."

"Y'all take that conversation someplace else," Papa said. "This is getting to be too much in here."

Mama and Miss May picked up their coffee cups. They

were heading to the living room when Mama turned around to me and whispered, "I'll be right back." That usually meant she was gonna try and get Miss May to leave soon. I just smiled at her.

"That's a nice thing Miss May is doin' by lettin' Billy, his sister, and their mother stay with her," I said to Papa.

"Yeah," Papa said. "That is nice. It's kinda hard for a lot of people right now."

"Papa, why is it that some people have jobs and others don't?" I asked, really not understanding. "I mean, Mom said that everyone should know they're too blessed to be stressed, but some people are so stressed that they have to steal stuff."

"Well, let me try to break this down the simplest way I can. A long time ago, you know us African Americans were slaves. Right?"

"Yes, Papa."

"Well, the African Americans worked for the slave owners. We didn't have anything—not even our own freedom. We've come a long way since then. Generations of faith and hard work helped us overcome, but as a people, we've still got issues to overcome. Even so, a lot of families have wealth because they inherit it. Do you know what the word *inherit* means?"

"Yes, sir. It means something that was passed down."

"Exactly. Well, a lot of African American families that never had anything in the first place couldn't pass down anything. They were poor and their parents were poor. If their kids didn't get a good education, they had a good chance of being poor too. You know, like how the weather says it's going to be a 90 percent chance of rain before it rains?"

"Yes, sir."

"Most African American kids who don't go to school have a 90 percent chance that they'll be poor, end up in jail, or stay on welfare their whole life."

Mama came into the room. "You all look like you're in a deep conversation. What are you talking about?"

"I'm explaining to Morgan why some people have the finer things in life and some don't."

I had been so into what everybody was talking about that I forgot to eat my breakfast. But the smell made me remember. So I started eating my French toast, eggs, and sausage. I was determined to finish this good food before it got any colder.

"Kids just have to understand that they need to go to school and learn. You can't go to school and act crazy. You won't learn anything that way. You've got to go to school to get your lesson. Whether or not parents have anything, education is the most important thing. The Lord is on our side, each one of us. We have to believe in Him and we have to work for what we need. People are not supposed to steal things that don't belong to them. Everybody should go to school and take advantage of all the **resources** that school has to offer."

"And that's why we're so proud of you, Morgan,"

Mama said. "You're getting your work done. That's what you're supposed to do. And make sure when your mom tells you not to take something to school that you mind her, you hear?"

"Yes, ma'am," I said. It tickled me when she kissed me on the cheek, and I laughed.

I loved them so much and they taught me so much. I knew they were in my life to guide me and that was a blessing.

•••••

On Sunday, Mama and Papa took me with them to church. I missed going to Greenforest Church. Mom and I used to attend with them before we started going to Daddy Derek's church. This morning I was really happy that I'd see all my old friends in Sunday school class. I liked the teacher, Miss Smith, too. And most of all, I missed my best friend, Joanie.

"I know everyone is excited to see Morgan, but I need you to settle down so we can go over the Ten Commandments. Like I told you last week, you can find them in the book of Deuteronomy. If you all have your Bibles, turn to chapter 6. Deuteronomy 6:7 says: "You shall teach them **diligently** to your children." Does anyone know what the Ten Commandments are?"

Joanie raised her hand and said, "Yes, it's the rules that God gave Moses for God's children to follow."

"That's exactly right. Now, most of us have heard of

the Ten Commandments and may understand some of them, but today we're going to go over them all. Like the Scripture says, it's important that you follow them diligently. That means putting all your might and your whole heart into it. If you don't follow God's rules then you'll live your life doing things that do not please Him. God has **parameters** set in place. Does anyone know what I mean by 'parameters'?"

Miss Smith waited for someone to answer, but no one raised their hand. Not even me. We all turned around and looked at each other until Miss Smith started talking again.

"That's okay, let me explain. Parameters are guidelines. They help set the direction that we are supposed to follow. The Ten Commandments are found in the book of Deuteronomy, chapter 5, verses 7 through 21."

Then Miss Smith began to explain them one by one.

"The first commandment says, 'You shall have no other gods before Me.' That basically means that the God of the Bible is the only God we must follow. Number two, 'You shall not make for yourself a carved image.' That means we should have no idols. A long time ago, people used to carve gods out of wood and stones and worship them. Today, an idol can be anything that people treat as more important than God in their lives. Number three, 'You shall not take the name of the Lord your God in vain.' Simply, honor God's name. Don't walk around saying, 'Oh, my God!' about everything."

We all started to laugh at that because so many people say that all the time.

Miss Smith clapped her hands to settle us down. "I'm serious. That is disrespectful and we are to honor God's name. Commandment number four, 'Observe the Sabbath day, to keep it holy.' On Sunday, you're supposed to rest, come to church, and worship the Lord. Number five, 'Honor your father and your mother.' Young people, this is one you should work on extra hard. You all know what it means. Obey your parents. You need their guidance. Listen to your parents because they know what's best for you."

I knew exactly what that meant now. I didn't wanna tell everyone about what happened, but I listened a lot and learned a lot. Miss Smith was right. We don't know it all. If I had listened to my mom, I would still have my iPod right now. All the stuff that had happened over the past week was bad news that wouldn't have happened.

"All right, number six, 'You shall not murder.' We are not supposed to take anyone's life. God wants us to value human life by taking care of one another."

This one made me think about how important my family is to me. I would be missing so much if Daddy, Mom, Mama, Papa, Daddy Derek, Jayden, and all my cousins were not in my life.

Miss Smith continued. "Number seven, 'You shall not commit adultery.' I see a lot of you guys looking confused. This is for grown-ups. It just means that when people get married they should only have a relationship with each other. Commandment eight, 'You shall not steal.' You all should know that it is wrong to take something that doesn't belong to you." Thinking about my iPod, I knew exactly what she was talking about. It made me wish Bridget was here to learn about it.

"Number nine, 'You shall not bear false witness against your neighbor.' This means do not tell lies. You have got to be honest, young people. Don't say that someone did something that they didn't do. Your words are important. If people can't trust what you say, they can't trust you. Lastly, number ten, 'You shall not covet.' That means don't be jealous of what someone else has."

Miss Smith finished the lesson by saying, "Those are the Ten Commandments. I challenge each and every one of you to learn them and keep them close to your heart. Do your best and live for God every day. Okay now, it's time to enjoy some snacks before we go up to the morning service."

We knew we didn't have much time, so all the kids hurried over to the table to grab a carton of milk and some butter cookies.

"How've you been, Morgan?" Joanie asked. "I see you hurt your head."

She was pointing to the bandage on my forehead. Although it wasn't hurting anymore, my stitches hadn't come out yet.

"It's a long story," I said.

"Well, we have to keep in touch. Maybe we can visit each other sometime."

"That'll be great."

"The Ten Commandments are great. Right? But, it's so much to learn."

"Yeah, it sure is."

When Joanie and I went up to the sanctuary, the place where we have church service, I found Mama and Papa. I was surprised to see Billy with Miss May, his sister Bridget, and their mom. The sermon for today was also about the Ten Commandments. The music was good and I understood most of the pastor's message. Then it was time for the pastor to invite anyone who was ready to come up and give their life to the Lord. Bridget surprised me when she got up and walked down the aisle.

I hadn't taken that big step yet. I did wanna be baptized one day. But I wasn't ready yet to give my life to Christ, even though I knew in my heart that it was the right thing to do.

Anyway, I guess Bridget was ready because she needed God right now. Her family was going through tough times and that was making her do tough things. She was suspended from school for a week. And I heard this wasn't her first time doing something like this. Bridget knew it was time for her to turn her life around.

When church was over, I was glad she came up to me. Before I could tell her how happy I was for her, she put her hands in her purse and pulled out something.

"Here's your iPod, Morgan. I'm sorry I stole it. I broke one of the Commandments. But I asked the Lord for forgiveness today and now I know I really need to ask for yours too. The other day I wasn't sincere, but you forgave me anyway. I just wanna know, was your forgiveness real even though I didn't deserve it?"

I just hugged her. And I guess that said it all. She could feel I was real. Sometimes actions are kind enough.

Letter to Dad

Dear Dad,

Hope you are okay off the coast of Africa, serving our country on that big ship. I miss you so much, Dad. Please come home soon!

We're doing reviews in school to get ready for the big test. I learned that a **passage** is a section of a letter, a poem, a story, or a report. I know that a letter should have a **salutation**, like Dear Dad. I know that a **scenario** is a situation or setting.

I **appreciate** my teacher, Mrs. Hardy, because she's helping us to learn so much and take advantage of our **resources**. We are **diligently** working hard in the computer labs and in the classroom. The biggest thing I've learned lately is that God gave us the Ten Commandments so we'd have **parameters** to live by. I'm working hard to please Him.

Your daughter,
Better Morgan

Word Search

```
C  O  R  D  C  H  O  R  D  F  O  D
T  H  O  A  R  S  E  O  V  E  R  I
A  P  P  R  E  C  I  A  T  E  T  L
S  A  L  U  T  A  T  I  O  N  R  I
H  D  P  L  E  D  L  E  A  D  E  G
O  P  A  R  A  M  E  T  E  R  S  E
R  E  S  W  R  I  T  E  P  E  O  N
S  R  S  R  I  G  H  T  M  D  U  T
E  H  A  I  R  H  A  R  E  R  R  L
Q  U  G  M  E  E  T  X  U  E  S  Y
U  K  E  M  E  A  T  J  D  A  E  Z
I  C  K  O  I  R  A  N  E  C  S  H
```

APPRECIATE

DILIGENTLY

PARAMETERS

PASSAGE

RESOURCES

SALUTATION

SCENARIO

Words to Know and Learn

1) **pas·sage** (păs′ĭj) *noun*
Part of a story, letter, poem, or report.

2) **sal·u·ta·tion** (săl′yə-tā′shən) *noun*
A word or phrase of greeting used to begin a letter or message.

3) **sce·nar·i·o** (sĭ-nâr′ē-ō′, -när′-, -năr′-) *noun*
An outline or summary of a play, movie, or book.

4) **ap·pre·ci·ate** (ə-prē′shē-āt′) *verb*
To be thankful or show gratitude for.

5) **re·source** (rē′sôrs′, -sōrs′) *noun*
Something that can be used for support or help.

6) **dil·i·gently** (dĭl′ə-jənt lē) *adverb*
Marked by steadily trying to reach a goal.

7) **pa·ram·e·ter** (pə-răm′ĭ-tər) *noun*
A boundary or limit.

Chapter 7

Added Charm

We were having a big spelling review test. Ugh. Miss Hardy had given us extra time in the classroom to study for it because it would have all the words we'd learned from the first four months of school.

Some of the words were tricky to learn. Like, the word *final* is different from the word *finally*, which is spelled *f-i-n-a-l-l-y*, with two *l*'s. *Beautiful* is spelled *b-e-a-u-t-i-f-u-l* and it is a different word than *beauty*. *Happiness* is spelled *h-a-p-p-i-n-e-s-s* and it is a different word than *happy*. There are certain rules that you have to know to spell these words correctly. And if you want to know the rules, then you have to study them.

Mrs. Hardy went to the office. Before she left, she told us we would have a few minutes to study for the test. But we would have to be ready to take it when she returned. I looked over at Brooke and she was shaking. She could barely sit still because she was so jumpy.

"Are you okay?" I asked her. "You look like you need to go and get some water."

"I said I was gonna do better and I was gonna study hard for my tests. But I'm so nervous."

"Why? Even though we have two hundred words, there's only gonna be twenty words on the test."

"Morgan, I understand that. But I don't know what words will be on the test. I'm not sure I studied enough."

"Why not? We've known about this test for two weeks."

She leaned over closer to me and said, "You gotta help me. Please. Just let me see your paper like I did on our times tables test."

I didn't say anything. We were finally best buddies again. So why would she ask me to do something wrong again? Brooke should know by now I couldn't help her like that.

I just kept looking at her. But she wasn't backing down or taking no for an answer. Brooke was trying to show me how far to lean my paper to the corner of my desk. She would move over just close enough to see my paper. My friend was determined and now I was shaking.

I knew what getting in trouble felt like. I knew how it would feel to let my mom down again. I knew that the Lord wanted me to honor His rules and laws. Although the Bible didn't come right out and say you're not supposed to cheat on a spelling test, I knew it was wrong.

I got up from my desk and went to the pencil sharpener. Thinking so hard about this, I just started to pray.

Lord, Brooke is asking me to help her again like I tried to do before. This time I just can't. I tried to study with her on the phone the other day but all she wanted to talk about was TV shows. I didn't even stay on the phone long with her because I knew I had to study. I put in my work and I shouldn't have to do extra. I know how to spell graceful, lovely, and Thursday. You helped me to get ready for this test. Now, can You give me the strength to tell Brooke no? I need Your help, Lord Jesus. Amen.

As soon as I sat back down, Mrs. Hardy walked through the door. "Okay, class. Now we can take a break and get some water before the test. Clear your desks and then we'll come back and take the test."

Everyone lined up quickly. I was glad that I was already by the door so I didn't have far to go. I forgot I had my pencil in my hand. Since I didn't want to lose my place in line and put the pencil back, I stuck it in my hair. I was so relieved that Brooke wasn't standing behind me. I needed this break away from her.

"I know you're not gonna help your friend," Alec said to me.

"And how do you know she needs help?" I asked. Not looking behind me, I kept walking.

"She was moving her paper around and you were looking upset. I know you're not gonna help her, right? Remember what happened last time when you almost got caught. If it wasn't for me saving you then, you would still be in trouble."

I turned around with one hand on my hip and said, "I can handle myself. Okay?"

Mrs. Hardy called out, "Morgan, please keep walking. You know there's silence in the line."

"Thanks a lot."

"Whatever. That's nothing compared to the trouble you'd be in for gettin' caught helpin' a cheater."

I huffed and headed into the girls' washroom. Ever since the **incident** that happened to me, I made it my business to be quick in the bathroom. As soon as I came out to wash my hands, Brooke was standing there waiting on me.

"So, you're gonna help me, right?" she pleaded.

I took her arm and pulled her over to the corner so no one else from our class would hear. "No, I'm not gonna help you."

I tried to walk away but she pulled me back and demanded, "Why not?"

"Because you should have studied and I don't wanna get caught tryin' to help you. Yes, you're my best friend. But like my mom said, if you were a true friend you would want to help me do the right thing rather than—"

Brooke cut me off and said, "Ugh. Spare me the best friend speech. I do what's right. You weren't sayin' that when you needed my help with the iPod story."

"And I was wrong. Look how that all turned out."

"Still, I'd help you do it all over again. Right now, I need you to help me. Why won't you, Morgan?"

"Because He won't let me," I said, as I pointed upward.

She stormed away and opened up the bathroom door so hard that it hit the wall and made Mrs. Hardy come and check on us. "Hurry up, girls, so you can take your test."

I went outside and got back in line. Alec was in front of me this time.

"I can tell you told her no. She's mad, but don't sweat it. She'll come around and be okay."

"I doubt it. Look at her with her arms folded at the front of the line. If she's gonna be mad at anybody then she needs to be mad at herself."

"My parents helped me learn how to keep my anger in check. And I had to pray and work on it on my own. If I can do it, I know she can work on herself. She'll be better for you not helpin' her."

"When did you become so smart?"

"I don't know. My dad's been having some man talks with me before I go to bed. He's helpin' me and my brother to see things from a different **perspective**."

"Perspective? Look at you using such a big word. I hope you know how to spell words like that on the test."

"I'll give it a good try. Perspective means a point of view."

"I know what it means, Alec. I was only joking. It's not gonna be on the spelling test."

"Oh, I forgot I was talking to Miss Smart, Morgan Love."

I tapped him lightly on the arm. I really appreciated him helping me feel better.

• • • • •

"Okay, Morgan. Your poster looks so lovely," Mom said, as she dropped me off at school.

Today was the day of the student council elections. I had my speech ready, my poster was ready, and I even brought some treats for the class to boost my votes. They were gonna vote and I wanted to win.

"Thanks to you, Mom, my poster is so cool," I said, proud of how it sparkled with bold words.

We had used colorful, neon markers to make my poster read:

You are going to LOVE
having MORGAN
as your
Student Council Representative!

"No, you're the one who made sure everything got done. You mixed blue coloring with the vanilla frosting to make blue cupcakes for the boys and mixed red coloring to make pink cupcakes for the girls," said Mom.

"I even made a special white cupcake for Trey because I know I'm running against him. Even if he wins, I won't be mad because he's my friend. That's okay, right? Billy said I'm supposed to have a backbone, but I don't know what that means."

"He's saying you need to be tough," Mom explained,

looking at me like she was real proud.

"Tough? Why would he say that?"

She kissed me on the forehead and said, "I don't know where he got that from, Morgan. But I do know that a good politician should have **compassion** and a caring heart for her **opponent**. You're going to do great today. As long as you do your best, you know I'm proud of you."

"Thanks, Mom. Oh, and thanks for helping me spell representative correctly. It would be a shame to have a word spelled wrong on my poster."

As soon as I got into the classroom, everyone rushed up to me. I guess it did help that I had fresh cupcakes in my hand. They looked yummy and everybody wanted one right away.

"No fair. You brought cupcakes!" Trey yelled out.

I shrugged my shoulders. "Of course, I brought cupcakes. Why isn't it fair?"

"I'm tellin' Mrs. Hardy. This isn't right," he said, still pouting.

I stood my ground and defended, "It is right. She told us to do something cool for the class."

"Yeah, Trey. Don't get mad because you don't have anything," Alec said. "Can I have a cupcake now, Morgan?"

I tugged the box away so no one could get in it. "Not now. You have to wait until I give my speech."

The class was up and about, going up and down the fifth grade hallway. They were all looking at the posters of everyone running for president and vice president. Even the fourth grade candidates running for secretary and treasurer had posters there too.

Since Trey and I were the only ones running from our class, Mrs. Hardy placed our posters right outside our door. The class swarmed over to them like they were bees on a honeycomb.

I really hoped that everyone thought my poster was cute. This was a time when I wished Brooke and I were cool with each other. I wanted to ask her if she liked my poster.

Brooke just looked at me and walked away. She was still upset about the spelling test. I had gotten an A+ and she got an F. I knew she was in trouble because when you make bad grades, your parents have to sign the test.

All of a sudden, I heard all this laughing going on over Trey's poster. People were pointing to something, so I made my way to see what they were laughing about. I saw that he had a word spelled wrong.

I hurried down the hall to find him. "Trey, you spelled council wrong."

"No, I didn't. You're just sayin' that so I can lose."

"No, really. The word *council* doesn't have an *e* on the end. It's spelled *c-o-u-n-c-i-l*."

"Just because you made a perfect score on the spelling test doesn't mean I spelled it wrong," Trey said.

I was trying to help him and he didn't believe me. I just don't understand friends sometimes. They get mad at you when you do the right thing. When you don't help them do something wrong, they get mad at you. And when you do the right thing to help them, they get mad. Whatever.

Later on in the day when it was time for the class to vote, I was called on first.

"Class, I know I'm not a perfect person, but I do want to represent you if given the chance. If I'm elected, I'd make sure every voice in this room gets heard. We are all special and I'd make sure you know that."

The class clapped. Even Brooke nodded and clapped for me. Seeing her smiling at me made me feel better than eating one of those cupcakes ever could.

When Mrs. Hardy called on Trey to speak, he stood up and said, "I've decided not to run. I think Morgan Love is the best person for the job. When everyone was laughing at me because I had a misspelled word on my poster, she didn't. She tried to help me. She tries to help all of us. She cares. Morgan should be our student representative."

And that was it! Mrs. Hardy took the votes after both of our speeches and the class **unanimously** voted for me. Wow! What an honor.

• • • • •

It was Saturday and Mom surprised me when she came into my room to ask if I wanted a play date with Brooke. I wasn't sure how I was going to tell her that Brooke and I weren't friends anymore. Even though she clapped for me in school the other day, we still weren't talking.

My mom, Brooke's mom, and Chanté's mom had given the three of us a big talk about how friends were supposed to get along, not talk about one another, and do right for each other. My mom just didn't know that I had tried all of that already with Brooke.

I didn't want her to feel bad for me, so I just said, "No, that's okay. If anything, I might call Chanté. I don't get to see her that much in school anymore. I'll see."

"So, why don't you want Brooke over?" Mom wasn't letting me go. "You know, Morgan, you can talk to me. That's if you want to. We can talk about friendships. The best friendships take a whole lot of work. I know you all are having problems."

"What? I didn't say anything. How did you know? It's not like I've been crying or anything about it."

"I can sense it. And plus, Brooke's mom called to tell me that Brooke has been crying about it."

"Really? At school, she won't even talk to me. I didn't think she cared."

"Well, it's bothering her. Her mom even told me what the problem was. And I just wanna say that I am so proud of you. You were right for not letting Brooke look on your paper. Brooke said that she knows that you were right too. And her mom wants to thank you for being her daughter's friend and standing up to her. She'd like to take the two of you someplace special today. Do you want to go?"

"I love Brooke, Mom, but sometimes she just complains

too much when she doesn't get her way. She's pretty and that gets her a lot of attention. So it makes her think she doesn't have to work as hard as some of us."

"Well, Morgan, you're precious too."

"Yes, I already know I'm cute, and I know I'm smart," I said in a little snippy tone.

"Morgan!"

"I'm sorry, Mom. I'm upset. I'm just sayin' that I wanna be Brooke's friend, but anytime I'm not doin' something that she likes, she just drops me. How much am I supposed to take? When I was gettin' a little attention because I was smart, she didn't wanna be my friend. When I told on Trey and she thought I was wrong for that, she turned her back on me again."

Mom could see how upset I was about it all, and it was making me feel better to tell her the whole story.

"And now that I didn't let her look at my paper, she doesn't want to be my friend again. I got in trouble for listening to her when we tried to watch that movie. I learned the hard way, but I was still her friend. I want her to be my friend, Mom, but I don't want to change who I am or have to feel bad because we can't get along."

"Well, why don't you hang out with her today and tell her that. Like I've said before, sweetie, friendships take work and it takes two people for it to succeed. If you're tired and fed up, I'm okay with that. But I believe deep down inside of you that you feel she is your best friend. If that's the case, tell her that you two have to work it out together."

"Yes, ma'am. I do want to go."

"Okay, you'd better hurry and get dressed. They'll be here in thirty minutes. I'll go and call her mom now."

An hour later, we arrived in a very nice area of Atlanta. Brooke's mom pulled up to a fancy place called a spa. I'd never been to a spa before. Yeah, I've heard of them because my mom goes from time to time to treat herself. But today was my time to enjoy myself and get pampered.

"Mrs. Atwater, thanks for bringing me. This is really great."

"You're welcome, dear. Before you girls get your nails done, I'm going to sit with you and Brooke in the relaxation room. It's a comfortable place where we can rest and chat."

Wearing our fluffy robes and slippers, we followed behind her. She and Brooke sat down on the pretty sofa and I sat in a big, comfy chair.

"Brooke has been **distraught** that you girls haven't been acting like friends lately. So today I wanted you to do something really special together. Morgan, I like the fact that the two of you are friends. You all should be closer, but Brooke told me that she hasn't been acting like a friend should."

I looked over at Brooke and tears were pouring from her eyes. I got out of my chair, walked over, and hugged her. I felt bad for her. When I was talking to my mom, I told her I was fed up with Brooke and all the changes she put me through. But her heart seemed so heavy right now. And when I looked in her eyes, I could tell she cared about me too.

"Mrs. Atwater." One of the service providers came in and said, "I'm ready to take you back for your facial. Someone will be here to get the girls in a few minutes."

"You girls talk. I'll see you in a while," said Mrs. Atwater.

"I'm so sorry, Morgan. I asked you to forgive me before, but I keep doing wrong things. You're always there to help me pick up the pieces. Thanks for being my friend. Mrs. Hardy is giving me a chance to retake the test and I think I learned some new words. It would be nice if you could go over them with me."

"You can ask your best friend anything," I said to her.

"You mean, you forgive me again?"

"I didn't know where we were going because my mom didn't say. It didn't have to be a spa. I would've come anyway to get our friendship back. I want us to be strong. You don't always have to think like me and I don't always have to think like you. But we must help each other do the right things. If we do that, we'll be okay."

"Well, I want to learn how to be accountable, Morgan," Brooke said, surprising me. "Maybe we can help each other make the right choices and do the right things. You know, God's way. When we first met, remember how we used to talk about stuff?"

"The only thing I can say to you is keep putting God first. You have to believe for yourself that He loves you and wants the best for you. When God is in our hearts that's when we can love others. We can do the right thing. We can be great people and we can have added **charm**."

Letter to Dad

Dear Dad,

The **incident** with the girl taking my iPod has finally been solved. I found out who it was and got a good **perspective** as to why Bridget did that. Dad, her family doesn't have their own home. And even though that's no reason to steal, I do have **compassion** for this girl.

Also, you know I was running for class representative. Well, my **opponent** dropped out because he said I deserved to win. The class voted for me unanimously.

Then I was **distraught** that my friend Brooke and I weren't acting like buddies. But we worked it out and said we'd stay good girls by showing class and **charm**. Thanks for praying for me, Dad.

Your daughter,
Representative Morgan

Word Search

```
N  D  O  P  P  E  L  R  A  D  U  H
P  I  N  C  I  D  E  N  T  A  N  O
E  S  D  H  L  V  A  P  K  R  A  W
R  T  I  E  W  Y  N  S  N  E  N  M
S  R  S  N  O  E  A  T  T  R  I  A
P  A  T  O  M  J  C  H  A  R  M  N
E  U  R  T  N  E  N  O  P  P  O  Y
C  G  A  B  U  R  G  E  R  I  U  W
T  H  U  R  H  D  O  W  N  S  S  R
I  T  G  N  Q  E  R  A  S  R  L  I
V  O  T  E  O  F  T  E  N  E  Y  T
E  I  C  O  M  P  A  S  S  I  O  N
```

CHARM

COMPASSION

DISTRAUGHT

INCIDENT

OPPONENT

PERSPECTIVE

UNANIMOUSLY

Words to Know and Learn

1) **in·ci·dent** (ĭn'sĭ-dənt) *noun*
An event.

2) **per·spec·tive** (pər-spĕk'tĭv) *noun*
A mental view or outlook.

3) **com·pas·sion** (kəm-păsh'ə) *noun*
Care for someone or something.

4) **op·po·nent** (ə-pō'nənt) *noun*
One that opposes another or others in a battle, contest, controversy, or debate.

5) **u·nan·i·mously** (yʊ-năn'ə-məs) *adverb*
In complete agreement.

6) **dis·traught** (dĭ-strôt') *adjective*
Deeply agitated, angry, or worried.

7) **charm** (chärm) *noun*
The attractive qualities of a personality.

1. Brooke spends the night and convinces Morgan to watch a movie her mom told them not to watch. Do you think Morgan should have followed her friend and watched the program anyway? When your friend tells you to do something you know is wrong, how can you stand up to her and do what's right?

2. When it's time for the test, Brooke wants to copy from Morgan's paper. Do you believe Morgan should be stressing about not helping her friend? Is helping a friend cheat ever the right thing to do?

3. Morgan notices that Alec is being very nice to her. Do you believe Alec is impressed by Morgan's faith? Do you ever think people notice how you act toward God?

4. When Morgan goes on a field trip, her mother tells her she cannot take her iPod. Do you think Morgan was wrong to take the music player on the trip anyway? Why do you think you should obey your parents?

5. When Morgan goes to the restroom two girls steal her iPod and she gets severely hurt trying to stop them. Do you feel Morgan learned her

lesson from disobeying her mom? Did you ever learn something the hard way?

6. Bridget, Billy's sister, is the girl who stole from Morgan. When she goes to church, do you think God can help make her life better? Do you believe God forgives us when we ask Him?

7. Morgan and Brooke were not speaking for a while because Brooke wanted Morgan to help her cheat. When Brooke asked Morgan once more to help her on a test, should Morgan have let her copy from her paper? Have you ever buckled down and told a friend that you weren't going to let them make you do the wrong thing?

Word Keep Book

Chapter 1: recommend, homophones, instincts, disobeyed, gritting, accountable, attention

Chapter 2: mandatory, integrity, tutoring, astute, reputation, eager, deserve

Chapter 3: antics, grateful, diversion, dictated, sacrificed, candidate, timid

Chapter 4: souvenirs, convincing, pondering, conscience, phenomenal, artifacts, blurry

Chapter 5: ecstatic, compress, liability, numbed, commandments, conference, arrogant

Chapter 6: passage, salutation, scenario, appreciate, resources, diligently, parameters

Chapter 7: incident, perspective, compassion, opponent, unanimously, distraught, charm

4 Bonus English Pages
Worksheet 1: Homophones

Homophones are words that sound alike. These words have different spellings and different meanings.

Example: pair and pear sound alike, but have different meanings.

This is a new _____ of shoes. (pair, pear)

Answer: pair

Have a slice of this delicious _____ . (pair, pear)

Answer: pear

Directions: Circle the correct word to complete the sentence. Then write the word on the line.

1. Morgan usually goes to bed at _____.
   (ate, eight)

2. Billy's _____ lets him stay up late. (ant, aunt)

3. Trey _____ everyone's food at lunch. (ate, eight)

4. Tim did not _____ what page we were on. (no, know)

5. Jayden has a _____ in his pacifier. (hole, whole)

6. Bridget needs to _____ her own iPod. (by, buy)

7. Alec asked to have _____ brownies with his milk.
   (to, two)

8. Antione _____ the race against his brother.
   (one, won)

9. My mom told me to _____ a jacket to school.
   (wear, where)

10. Brooke's favorite story is the "Tortoise and the _____."
    (Hair, Hare)

132

Worksheet 2: Contractions

A contraction is a shortened form of a word or words.

Examples:

do not: don't

can not: can't

would not: wouldn't

Example:

Billy wasn't eating any of the cake.

Answer: <u>wasn't</u>; was not

Directions: Underline the contraction in each sentence. Then, write the words that each contraction stands for.

1. I don't understand what Mrs. Hardy is saying. _____
2. She'll come over Mama's house. _____
3. Trey could've gone to the football game. _____
4. Billy shouldn't talk with his mouth full. _____
5. You and Brooke haven't seen the movie yet, right?_____
6. I'll be going to get ice cream with Papa. _____
7. Sorry, Alec can't come out and play. _____
8. I won't be home until after school. _____
9. She's gone to the playground already. _____
10. Mom and Daddy Derek weren't in the kitchen. _____

Worksheet 3: Action Verbs

An action verb is a word that shows what someone or something is doing.

Examples:

Morgan sleeps on the couch sometimes.

Answer: sleeps

Trey's best friend helped him make a poster.

Answer: helped

Alec and his mother cook dinner together.

Answer: cook

Directions: Circle the action verb in each sentence below.

1. Brooke listens to her favorite song on her iPod.
2. Trey kicks the ball over the fence.
3. Little baby Jayden grunts a lot.
4. The roof on the house leaks.
5. Mrs. Hardy searches for her chalk.
6. The school nurse examines Morgan.
7. The bluebird in the tree sings so beautifully.
8. The boys dash out of the classroom.
9. Morgan reads a book each night.
10. Mama buys ice cream at the store.

Worksheet 4: Subjects and Predicates

Every complete SENTENCE **contains two parts: a** SUBJECT **and a** PREDI-CATE. **The subject is what (or who) the sentence is about, and the predicate tells something about the subject.**

Example: The teacher told us to sit down.

Subject: the teacher; predicate: told us to sit down

Directions: Underline the subject and circle the predicate in the sentences below.

1. The gardener planted flowers.
2. The pilot flew the airplane.
3. The little puppy barked all night long.
4. The barber cut Trey's hair.
5. Morgan's baby brother slept in his crib.
6. The flag blew in the wind.
7. The lizard ate crickets.
8. The plumber fixed the sink.
9. The bus driver drove me to school.
10. The teacher taught us a lesson.

Chapter 1 Solution

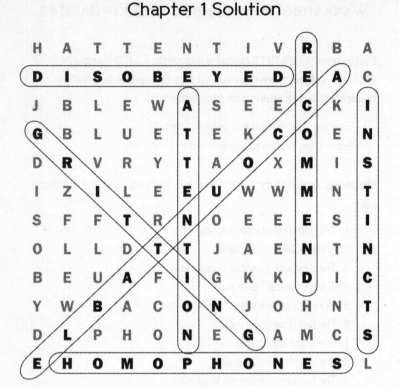

ACCOUNTABLE

ATTENTION

DISOBEYED

GRITTING

HOMOPHONES

INSTINCTS

RECOMMEND

Chapter 2 Solution

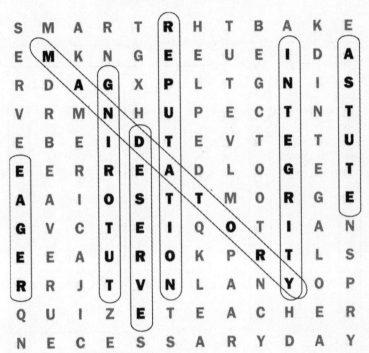

```
S  M  A  R  T  T  R  H  T  B  A  K  E  E
E  M  K  N  G  E  E  U  E  I  D  A
R  D  A  G  X  P  L  T  G  N  I  S
V  R  M  N  H  U  P  E  C  T  N  T
E  B  E  I  D  T  E  V  T  E  T  U
E  E  R  R  E  A  D  L  O  G  E  T
A  A  I  O  S  T  M  O  R  I  G  E
G  V  C  T  E  I  Q  O  T  I  A  N
E  E  A  U  R  O  K  P  R  T  L  S
R  R  J  T  V  N  L  A  N  Y  O  P
Q  U  I  Z  E  T  E  A  C  H  E  R
N  E  C  E  S  S  A  R  Y  D  A  Y
```

ASTUTE

DESERVE

EAGER

INTEGRITY

MANDATORY

REPUTATION

TUTORING

Chapter 3 Solution

```
X  C  A  N  D  I  D  H  S  O  R  E
D  B  E  P  D  I  C  T  A  T  E  D
I  J  S  C  H  O  O  G  C  I  M  A
C  G  G  A  N  S  L  R  R  M  O  N
T  R  R  N  C  B  P  A  I  E  R  O
A  E  A  D  O  R  M  T  F  D  G  I
N  A  T  I  D  Y  I  E  Y  W  A  S
T  T  E  D  I  N  Q  F  J  K  N  R
I  R  B  A  V  O  R  U  I  D  M  E
C  E  W  T  E  E  W  L  N  C  H  V
S  Y  K  E  R  L  N  A  V  Y  E  I
A  L  E  C  S  L  E  T  I  M  I  D
```

ANTICS

CANDIDATE

DICTATED

DIVERSION

GRATEFUL

SACRIFICED

TIMID

Chapter 4 Solution

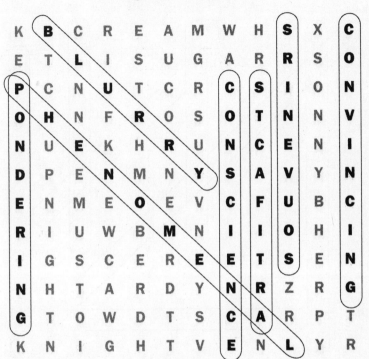

```
K  B  C  R  E  A  M  W  H  S  X  C
E  T  L  I  S  U  G  A  R  R  S  O
P  C  N  U  T  C  R  C  S  I  O  N
O  H  N  F  R  O  S  O  T  N  N  V
N  U  E  K  H  R  U  N  C  E  N  I
D  P  E  N  M  N  Y  S  A  V  Y  N
E  N  M  E  O  E  V  C  F  U  B  C
R  I  U  W  B  M  N  I  I  O  H  I
I  G  S  C  E  R  E  E  T  S  E  N
N  H  T  A  R  D  Y  N  R  Z  R  G
G  T  O  W  D  T  S  C  A  R  P  T
K  N  I  G  H  T  V  E  N  L  Y  R
```

ARTIFACTS

BLURRY

CONSCIENCE

CONVINCING

PHENOMENAL

PONDERING

SOUVENIRS

Chapter 5 Solution

```
C  C  E  A  N  T  U  B  T  C  T  R
C  O  J  L  L  N  Y  C  R  O  S  L
S  M  N  M  A  A  U  G  H  M  E  I
P  M  C  F  R  G  A  M  O  P  L  A
G  A  P  A  E  O  F  E  B  R  T  B
H  N  R  Q  U  R  T  O  R  E  P  I
E  D  E  O  K  R  E  B  E  S  D  L
T  M  E  O  K  A  E  N  E  S  D  I
T  E  S  C  N  A  J  N  C  S  P  T
T  N  K  I  X  S  O  S  C  E  P  Y
I  T  C  I  T  A  T  S  C  E  R  Y
F  S  M  E  A  T  B  A  L  L  S  J
```

ARROGANT

COMMANDMENTS

COMPRESS

CONFERENCE

ECSTATIC

LIABILITY

NUMBED

Chapter 6 Solution

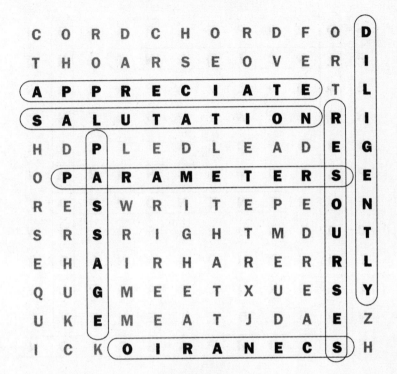

APPRECIATE

DILIGENTLY

PARAMETERS

PASSAGE

RESOURCES

SALUTATION

SCENARIO

Chapter 7 Solution

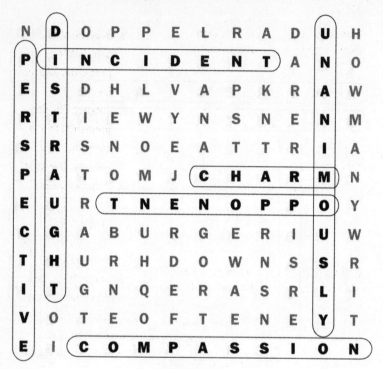

CHARM

COMPASSION

DISTRAUGHT

INCIDENT

OPPONENT

PERSPECTIVE

UNANIMOUSLY

Answer Keys

**Homophones
Worksheet 1**

1. eight
2. aunt
3. ate
4. know
5. hole
6. buy
7. two
8. won
9. wear
10. Hare

**Contractions
Worksheet 2**

1. don't; do not
2. she'll; she will
3. could've; could have
4. shouldn't; should not
5. haven't; have not
6. I'll; I will
7. can't; can not
8. won't; will not
9. she's; she has
10. weren't; were not

**Action Verbs
Worksheet 3**

1. listens
2. kicks
3. grunts
4. leaks
5. searches
6. examines
7. sings
8. dash
9. reads
10. buys

**Subject and Predicate
Worksheet 4**

1. **subject:** The gardener; **predicate:** planted flowers
2. **subject:** The pilot; **predicate:** flew the airplane
3. **subject:** The little puppy; **predicate:** barked all night long
4. **subject:** The barber; **predicate:** cut Trey's hair
5. **subject:** Morgan's baby brother; **predicate:** slept in his crib
6. **subject:** The flag; **predicate:** flew in the wind
7. **subject:** The lizard; **predicate:** ate crickets
8. **subject:** The plumber; **predicate:** fixed the sink
9. **subject:** The bus driver; **predicate:** drove me to school
10. **subject:** The teacher; **predicate:** taught us a lesson

Acknowledgments

So I caught my daughter on the phone when she was NOT supposed to be on it. She'd already made a bad decision to chat when she shouldn't have been on the phone, then when I asked her about it she wanted to tell a fib. She knew admitting the truth would land her in deep trouble, but she also knew telling me an untruth would be much, much worse.

Thankfully, she was smart and did the right thing and admitted her mistake. We talked about her bad choice. I hope she has learned to not disobey and is off punishment by the time you read this. The point is, we all make mistakes. We all get tempted to take the easy way out. We all think from time to time that it is better to act on wrong choices.

However, the Bible is God's law. He expects His people to obey Him. Your parents may seem harsh sometimes, but they do what they do because they have your best interest at heart. So tell them you love them, study hard, be sweet, and keep on making right choices.

I made a right choice to allow great people to help me write for you.

To my parents, Dr. Franklin and Shirley Perry, I want to say thank you for doing the right thing by raising me God's way.

For my Moody/Lift Every Voice Team, especially Roslyn Jordan, I want to say thank you for knowing that the right thing to do in pushing this book is a great marketing strategy.

For my sweet cousin and assistant, Ciara Roundtree, and my brother and his family, Dennis Perry, Leslie Perry, and Franklin Perry, I want to say thank you for giving me your time and always being there.

For my friends who gave input into this series, Sarah Lundy, Jenell Clark, Vanessa Davis Griggs, Carol Hardy, Lois Hardy, Veronica Evans, Sophia Nelson, Laurie Weaver, Taiwanna Brown-Bolds, Lakeba Williams, Jackie Dixon, Vickie Davis, Kim Monroe, Jan Hatchett, Veida Evans, Toi Willis, and Deborah Bradley, I want to say thank you so much for saying the right thing by giving me correct advice.

For my children, Dustyn Leon, Sydni Derek, and Sheldyn Ashli, I want to say thank you for doing the right thing and obeying your dad and me.

For my husband, Derrick Moore, I want to say thank you for doing the right thing by working hard for our family.

For my new young readers, I want to say thank you for doing the right thing by taking time to read, learn, and grow.

And to my Savior Jesus Christ, I want to say thank You for choosing to do the right thing by dying on the cross for all our sins.

A+ Attitude

ISBN-13: 978-0-8024-2263-7

Morgan is mad at the world because she can't have things her way. If she received a grade for her attitude it would be an F. When her mommy gets really sick Morgan realizes how mean she's been. She makes up her mind to have an A+ attitude no matter what.

LiftEveryVoiceBooks.com
MoodyPublishers.com

SPEAK UP

ISBN-13: 978-0-8024-2264-4

Morgan is not sure what to do when she discovers that Alec, the new kid, is bullying her cousin and kids at school. She becomes worried when her friend Trey starts hanging out with and acting like Alec. When Trey brings a knife to school, Morgan decides to speak up.

LiftEveryVoiceBooks.com
MoodyPublishers.com

No Fear

ISBN-13: 978-0-8024-2267-5

When Morgan tells her mommy about all the things that she's been afraid of and worrying about lately, including dying, her mommy tells her about the good news from God and about heaven. Morgan begins to understand why her parents and grandparents are always telling her to have no fear.

LiftEveryVoiceBooks.com
MoodyPublishers.com

SOMETHING SPECIAL

ISBN-13: 978-0-8024-2265-1

After getting in trouble for teasing her classmates at school and disappointing her parents, Morgan goes to vacation Bible school and learns that God made each person the way they are for a reason. She realizes that she and even those kids she'd teased at school are all okay just the way they are because God made them, and to Him they are all something special.

LEVB
LIFT EVERY VOICE BOOKS

LiftEveryVoiceBooks.com
MoodyPublishers.com

MAKING THE TEAM

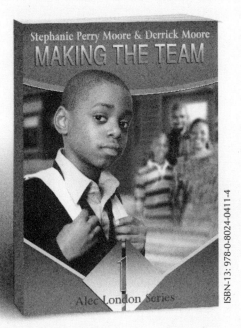

ISBN-13: 978-0-8024-0411-4

The Alec London Series is a series written for youth, 8-12 years old. Alec London is introduced in Stephanie Perry Moore's previously released series, *The Morgan Love Series*. In this new series, readers get a glimpse of Alec's life up close and personal. The series provides moral lessons that will aid in character development, teaching youth, especially boys, how to effectively deal with the various issues they face at this stage of life. The series will also help youth develop their English and math skills as they read through the stories and complete the entertaining and educational exercises provided at the end of each chapter and in the back of the book.

LiftEveryVoiceBooks.com
MoodyPublishers.com

OTHER BOOKS IN THE SERIES:

LEARNING THE RULES
GOING THE DISTANCE
WINNING THE BATTLE
TAKING THE LEAD

Lift Every Voice Books

Lift every voice and sing
Till earth and heaven ring,
Ring with the harmonies of Liberty;
Let our rejoicing rise
High as the listening skies,
Let it resound loud as the rolling sea.
Sing a song full of the faith that the dark past has taught us,
Sing a song full of the hope that the present has brought us,
Facing the rising sun of our new day begun
Let us march on till victory is won.

The Black National Anthem, written by James Weldon Johnson in 1900, captures the essence of Lift Every Voice Books. Lift Every Voice Books is an imprint of Moody Publishers that celebrates a rich culture and great heritage of faith, based on the foundation of eternal truth—God's Word. We endeavor to restore the fabric of the African-American soul and reclaim the indomitable spirit that kept our forefathers true to God in spite of insurmountable odds.

We are Lift Every Voice Books—Christ-centered books and resources for restoring the African-American soul.

For more information on other books and products written and produced from a biblical perspective, go to www.lifteveryvoicebooks.com or write to:

Lift Every Voice Books
820 N. LaSalle Boulevard
Chicago, IL 60610
www.lifteveryvoicebooks.com